Death's Twisted Tales

A Collection of Award Winning Short Stories

by

J.J. White

ISBN-13: 978-0615861616
ISBN-10: 061586161X

Dedication

To my beautiful and understanding wife, Pam.

Table of Contents

Author's Note

This book is a collection of short stories all revolving around the death theme. Once a short story has won an award or has been sold or has been published there is very little you can do with it other than bundle it with similar stories and publish it as a book. And so I did.

I would like to apologize for Death, or as he prefers, The Grim Reaper. When I contracted with him he agreed to promote and introduce these stories with what I assumed would be a positive slant. Instead, he takes every opportunity to criticize not only the stories but my style of writing. It's too late now, though. He's done his damage to the book and my reputation, but you can be sure he'll never work for me again. Unless he insists. He can be intimidating with that scythe and all.

As noted on the cover, there is a one-year guarantee that comes with the book. If you die within one year of purchase the author will cheerfully refund your money. A copy of the death certificate is necessary for the refund. If from the Afterlife, please e-mail or fax.

Author contact information:

e-mail: ebgb1022@cfl.rr.com

Website: http://www.jjwhite.webs.com/

Blog: http://jjdwhite.blogspot.com/

Acknowledgments

Special thanks to my mentors and gentle critics, Mary Brotherton, Athena Sasso, Hank Rhodes, and Matt Frakes. Thanks also to my brother Eddie.

ʄoreword

by The Grim Reaper

"Every story ends in death if one waits long enough."

The above quote is attributed to one of my employers, Beelzebub, who like myself, realizes everyone born will eventually die. My occupation is to collect or harvest the dead and deliver them to a clearinghouse where, depending on the situation, they will spend eternity in the pleasant confines of what you call Heaven, or they will fight the fires of Hell under the watchful eye of the previously mentioned said employer.

There is a common misconception that only Roman Catholics may enter the Pearly Gates while all others must reside in the sterility of Limbo. Of course this misconception is in fact championed by the Roman Catholics and is quite untrue. All can end, as Dante predicted, in *Paridiso*, *Purgatorio*, or *Inferno*.

So why, you ask, do I not wait until all are old and ready to leave the living instead of snatching some from all generations, infant to elderly? Simple. My employers, above and below, are easily bored and need the vigor of youth as well as the reticent submission of the old to keep the afterlife interesting. I have written a poem of explanation. I suggest you read it as it may be the only writing of interest in this book.

A poem by Death:

MORTALITY

Stay back death . . .

I won't stay back, come see your tomb
I've chased you since your mother's womb
You're no different at this dance
You've lasted longer just by chance

I chase them all right from the start
A newborn babe gives up its heart
Others run, through youth, but stumble
I'll take them too, not fair nor humble

Through middle age, a slowing down
Edging close, I reach around
Catching most in autumn years
When time and age cast off their fears

Everything and everyone
Must end it when their time is done
Life is like a river ride
Enjoy its ebb and flow of tide

But so it falls into the sea
So must you, my friend, you'll see
So yield your life, let's close the door
We must make room . . . room for more

The following tales are by J.J. White who surpasses his lack of literary talent only by his absence of writing skill. So why is it, you ask, do I, magnificent Death, The Grand Grim Reaper, belittle myself by agreeing to introduce each inane, incredulous story?

Simple. All of the following short stories have a happy ending.

Someone dies.

Rat Baiting

First Place winner of the Arizona Mystery Writers 2013 Short Story Competition

"I fondly remember the thousands of rats populating the sewers of London during those wonderful plague years of the sixteenth century. Twenty thousand fine residents of the fair city followed me on their journey from the living to the dead, most delivered to Hell, save some children and a few maidens. Busy as I was, it was a lovely time, thanks to my vermin friends.

In our story, the nineteenth century is coming to an end and young Fredrick Begley also finds himself fascinated with the large brown rats of London, though only when wagering on them in their death matches against stalwart terriers in the Rat Baiting arenas throughout the city. He cheers alongside the other fine gentlemen of the city as the muscular pit bulls rip the vermin to shreds.

Rats follow our protagonist throughout the story weaving in and out of the poor fool's life as does a certain genteel lady. Perhaps one would think Freddie to have better luck with her than the rats. Perhaps. Read for yourself to find out."

~ G.R.

From very close up I realized a rat, albeit a small one, could be considered attractive, with its pointed nose, bouncing whiskers, and tiny exposed teeth. I was not frightened when the rodent curiously examined me, as I, in turn, examined it.

It was yesterday I encountered similar said rodents though I was some distance from them then. I had just exited a hansom cab at an apartment house on the corner of Regent and Piccadilly, there to visit my longtime friend and companion Jonathan Davies-Taylor, when, during my attempt to avoid manure piles on the pediment, three aggressive rats popped their snouts out a sewer grate to observe the commotion I had made. Disgusting creatures—from a distance.

The occasion of my visit was a joyful one for two reasons.

One, I was there to congratulate my friend on his upcoming marriage to a beautiful maiden from Leeds. And two, to make plans for the upcoming New Year's celebration where all of London would welcome the arrival of the twentieth century.

Jonathan had written much about the mysterious and beautiful Miss Olivia Shaw, an orphan whose parents died a few years back while touring India, crushed by an elephant or some such nonsense that usually prevails in tales from the colony, never to be truly believed. In all likelihood, the young maiden's parents died, as so many others had, the victims of malaria, the elephant story, of course, so much more interesting in soirees. Still, Miss Shaw came with a sizeable dowry, and if her appearance in any way fit Davies-Taylor's description of her, he was indeed a lucky man.

This brings me to another reason for my visit that I had forgotten to mention. I was in need of one hundred and eighty pounds which I had lost to some rather suspect gentlemen at an eastside rat-baiting where I believe they had drugged the rats, allowing a fine terrier the freedom to kill all twenty-two vermin. I, unfortunately, had wagered on the rats. I was hoping Jonathan would be in such fine spirits that he would gladly part with, say, two hundred pounds for his best man and childhood friend.

The butler frowned as he took my coat, hat and cane. I will admit, my reputation with the Davies-Taylor help had never been satisfactory, the class separation between Jonathan and me the obvious reason. I cared not as I was young, intelligent and clever.

Bouncing into the foyer came Jonathan pulling his fiancée with him as a child would pull a toy wagon.

"Freddie!" he exclaimed. "Welcome, Freddie." He hugged me as if it had been years instead of months since we had last seen one another. He stepped aside and presented the most ravishing beauty, I believe, in all of London, perhaps all of England. My eyes were immediately drawn to her ample bosom and thin waist, for I am but a man after all. Jonathan swept his arm in a wide arc before this beauty and emoted.

"This, my dear friend, is the wonderful girl I have written to you of. May I present the lovely and soon to be Mrs. Jonathan Davies-Taylor. Olivia Shaw. Tell me Freddie, is she not everything I said she was?"

"And more," I said, taking her delicate pale hand and perhaps kissing it longer than proper. I looked up to her mesmerizing green eyes to voice something flirtatious and clever when our gazes locked for what seemed an interminable amount of time. Our jaws dropped and held in recognition.

"My God, it's you," I said forgetting Jonathan shared the same room.

"You know one another," he said. "Oh how grand. And I spent the day wondering if you would favor each other's company. How grand."

She mouthed two words to me.

"Say—nothing."

Say nothing? Say nothing? Was she insane? Did she think I would keep my knowledge of her identity from a boyhood chum? From a dear friend who could determine my future? Oh no, she was mistaken. My companion would not, will not be deceived by the likes of her. No sir, not Fredrick Begley's companion.

She turned to Jonathan, caressing his arm, pressing those marvelous breasts against his shoulder, her eyes, two green emeralds of passion and want.

"Dear, Jonathan. We are unacquainted, but I must have a word with your wonderful Freddie; just a moment to discuss secretive plans of bachelor festivities and gifts to her betrothed."

Jonathan's eyes darted from me to the wench and then back to me so many times I thought I'd pummel him to make him stop. "Oh my dear, you are the epitome of grace and knowledge. I shall leave you, but only as long as my heart can fathom the separation." He pointed at me. "You, sir. I assume you will treat this lovely goddess with the due respect and dignity she deserves."

I bowed. "But of course, Jonathan, though you may wish to say your good byes now to her as I am sure she will succumb to my wit and charm, as do all beautiful women."

Jonathan playfully punched my arm.

"Go. Off with you to the parlor. I will have Wallace close the room off and keep the curious ears of the help away. I expect great things from your secretive plans, my darling." He kissed the jezebel's lovely hand. "Great things."

With that, he left us. The accordion doors closed and then Miss Shaw peeked out to assure privacy. Satisfied, she sat across from me, a small table separating intimates. She once again froze me with her eyes.

"I am not her," she whispered.

"You are not?" I asked, keeping my voice level and sure. Men do not whisper.

"Please, I beg of you," she continued. "We must not be overheard."

I lighted one of the fine cigars from the table, testing Miss Shaw's patience, to be sure.

"And who are you if you are not you?" I said cleverly.

"I am myself, Olivia Shaw. The woman you think I am is my twin sister."

Oh, I had a hearty laugh at that which must have rattled the walls of the large apartment house.

"Please," she pleaded. "It is true, all of it. Her name is Anna and I dare not tell Jonathan of her. Why, the scandal would kill him, and you, also sir, might feel some of the effects. They are merciless as you well know. Society would castigate, he'd be a pariah throughout London."

I truly felt like applauding. It was a performance worthy of the Abbey Theatre, where I believe she may have spent some time.

"My God, girl," I said. "Do you think a man who has seen you naked and had you calling out his name in pleasure would not recognize his harlot? Oh, perhaps an ordinary whore but not one of your beauty and—" I stared at her heaving breasts, the cleavage parting and closing with rapid breaths. "and—your other attributes."

She stood, flustered, walking hurriedly to the fireplace, in all likelihood to draw me farther from the doors and the large ears of servants. I followed her as a fancy. She turned quickly to face me, the green of her eyes radiant in the glow of the crackling fire.

"It is true what I say, sir. I saw that look in your eye that I had seen so many times in all who had paid for her services and confused me with her, but it is true. I say that on the life of my future children. You mustn't tell him."

"It is true you say, Miss Shaw? No, that is the lie of a Leeds's whore." I pushed her roughly against the wall and debated between smashing her or ravishing her, the warmth and smell of her firm body exciting me as I pressed against her. She let out a muffled yell.

"Miss," the butler inquired through the thin door. "Is everything all right, Miss?"

"Yes," she said too loudly. "I—I dropped the candy dish, Wallace. Everything is fine. We won't be a moment."

"Yes, Miss."

I pressed harder with my body. Had she worn pants as in our last meeting, instead of the petticoated dress that wrinkled under my weight, I could not have stopped myself.

"You say you are Olivia, then?"

"Yes."

"Then why have you not called out for help? I take advantage of you, sweet Olivia, and you remain silent."

She had no answer. I grabbed her open neckline and pulled it forcefully exposing a good deal of her left breast. I pointed to a two inch scar, barely visible, but there all the same.

"And does your identical twin sister have an identical scar? Did you think I could forget you? Do you think any man could, Maggie?"

I released her and sat back in my seat. I had made my point. She shoved her breast back in place and straightened her dress. The innocent face had changed, still beautiful, though now stern and sure of will. It was Maggie the businesswoman who now sat across from me. It was time to start negotiations.

"You remembered me," I said. "How is that, my dear Maggie, amongst all those, how shall I put it, gentlemen?"

"Jesus, Mary, and Joseph, how could I forget you, me bruises and cuts still fresh in me head, you arrogant bastard. The things you did, you should be the one ta fear the constabulary."

"Ah, now that is the Maggie I spent a week's wages on. Shall I call Jonathan in to enlighten him, perhaps?"

Maggie grabbed my cigar from the table and took several puffs. Mulling it over in her Irish head, I believe.

"What is it you want, Freddie?"

I stood and paced a bit. "Not much. Not much. For the time being I am in need of two hundred pounds. I came here with every intention of asking my good friend—my very good friend, the loan of the amount until I could win back my losses but lo, now I find I am indeed in a position to ask that same favor of you, my love, although I shan't think we will consider it a loan. Let us call it a start, shall we?"

"Tomorrow—at seven," she said. "In Green Park, at the reservoir. Alone. I'll have your bloody money."

She stood and flung open the parlor doors. Much to my surprise, no one was there listening. How wonderful.

The next evening I waited until fifteen minutes past the seven o'clock before deciding to give up and leave. Then I felt an arm slip beneath mine. She smelled of lilac and smiled in the gaslight of the path as we walked. I patted her hand and smiled back. I pointed to an Art Nouveau bag that hung from her shoulder.

"The clothing?"

"Boy's pants, boy's shirt and a little sailor hat for I know you fancy little girls in little boy's sailor hats. Would you want a peek?"

"I will trust you, Maggie. My money?"

Maggie handed me a stack of twenty pound notes. I placed them in my jacket without counting and enjoyed the walk. "I have a friend with a flat nearby," I said. "It is ours for the night, and available in the future." I was in a wonderful mood and desired an invigorating conversation with my little nymph. "Shall we discuss your fortunate acquaintance with the distinguished Mr. Davies-Taylor? How did a woman of such ill-repute fall into the arms of such a man?"

"I gave up the business two years ago last month," she started. "Because of me looks, you know, I could charge more than the other Leeds girls and so I made a pretty penny for five years starting when I was fourteen, I was. But I wasn't like the others, Freddie. I saved every pence and banked it all, some even in your bloody bank."

I laughed. "My bank? Under what name, my dear?"

"What in hell name do you think? Olivia Shaw. It was to be my dowry. It is my dowry. I was set to meet a gentleman and make a new life of it. I was and I will. By the time I met Jonathan, I was well established in London as an orphan with an inheritance from me poor Da and Ma."

"Yes. They met their unfortunate demise under the weight of an elephant, I believe. Wonderful story. And the real da and ma?"

"In Cork. Living well and knowing it all, from the whoring to the orphan maiden. Why, they're a happy couple."

"I see," I said. "And now I have ruined it for you, have I not?"

"That you have, Freddie. And I only know you by your perversions, though I can imagine you'll be wantin' more money and more of me and God knows what, I think. Am I believing right?"

"You are, indeed. I shall need much of everything to seal my lips and keep clandestine the secrets of the fallen lass, the elegant Mrs. Davies-Taylor. As they say, we shall forge a wonderful relationship, both commercial and personal."

"Then that's it," she said. "And the good of it is that we're here."

"And where is here?" I said. It seemed I had lost track of our walk as we had stopped under a small bridge that was both musty and dark.

I spun her around and held her against the rock wall that formed part of the archway. Alone, as we were, I could see an advantage. I snaked my hand between petticoats and kissed her roughly on her lips.

"My little sailor," I said, forcing another kiss.

"But, sir," she said. "My friends."

"What friends?" I said, and kissed her again. She turned her head away.

"Jim and Bill."

"And who are Jim and Bill?"

"Why, Freddie. They are gentlemen from the place of my previous employment. They kept the clients in line and now they work for me."

I heard the cartilage snap in my nose as the shadow of a fist slammed into it with such force that I fell back on my haunches into a morass of mud. The two large men, Jim and Bill, I assume, lifted me like a small doll and proceeded to break what seemed to me every bone I had, one at a time, slowly, while covering my mouth with meaty hands to muffle my screams. They were quite thorough and left me lying in the mud and water with just a few short breaths left to breathe of the foggy London air.

I turned my head to watch the lovely Maggie walk daintily down the path upon which we came, her magnificent frame the silhouette of a Parisian hourglass.

A curious rat ventured out of the shadows to ascertain the strange lump that lay near its lair. I smiled a bloody toothless grin at the little bugger. It smiled in return.

Butterfly Tattoo

Honorable Mention Writers Digest *Crime Story Competition 2012*

"If asked what the greatest causes of death are, I would have to list war first, then sickness, and then, finally, and the most interesting, love. So many have met their maker (and me) in the name of love.

Alfred is much older than Candy. Alfred is married. Alfred has children. Candy has a butterfly tattoo and a boyfriend who's an ex-con. I think you have a pretty good idea that this relationship is not going to turn out well. Not well at all. At least I'm hoping it won't.

Though the characters are rather shallow and one dimensional, I believe it is worth reading just to see a naïve and boring actuary get his comeuppance.

No one likes actuaries."

~ G.R.

Alfred didn't think of himself as a bad man but as a good man who did some very bad things. Men do bad things for love. People do bad things for love, and Alfred was in love with the most exciting, beautiful, fabulous girl in the world, Candy Metzer.

He shoved it into drive and drove slowly out of the bank parking lot. It was his last stop of the day until his rendezvous with Candy at the "While-A-Way Motel," three hundred and twenty-two miles away from the Second National Bank and twelve point six miles west of Reno.

There was no need to look over his computer printout of the directions. Once he left the outskirts of the city, he only had to remember two roads, one, interstate, the other, state. It would take five hours and thirteen minutes to arrive at the motel, including frequent stops to urinate, fill up with gas, and even pause for a snack.

Alfred prided himself in his exactness. He planned everything in his life down to the minute, a necessity for an actuary. His obsession with accuracy was ingrained in his personality and perhaps that was why he was smitten with the wild, carefree, damn everything but the circus, Candy, with her marvelous outlook on life. She was his opposite.

Why him? He wasn't attractive, just the reverse, he looked the part of an actuary, short, nearly bald, no chest, and hips like a bowling pin. Yet she chose him. Why? Oh, who cared why, she did. She loved him. She said it sweetly in his ear as they lay in his and Rebecca's four-poster that he stole from Sears for half-price one Labor Day.

Rebecca. Dear Rebecca. She would be upset. Very upset. And then there were the children.

* * *

Candy crossed her eyes, then closed them for a moment, the white lines on the pavement starting to meld into just one, long, white one. She needed to pull over and crash for a while but if she did, and she was late, Jimbo would make her pay, like he always did.

Instead, she took a pinch of coke from a baggie and placed it in a line on top of her left hand, while continuing to steer the car with her knees. She sucked it in her sore, red nostrils in one quick sniff. It reminded her of her daddy snorting snuff, years ago, the mean son-of-a-bitch. She hoped he was in Hell with her momma. And, if there actually was a Hell, Candy would probably join them in a few years, the way she went through the Colombian pure.

The amp she took four hours earlier had run its course and that's why she needed the coke. Besides, it was the only way she could stay awake. Once they took care of Alfred at the "Whatever the hell it was Motel," she could sleep in Jimbo's car on the trip to Vegas. She shivered goose bumps as a combination of the coke kicking in and the image of Jimbo's perfect pecs improved her mood.

It would be dusk soon and she didn't like driving at night. Why hadn't Jimbo set this up close to home? She knew why. Jimbo wanted to blow some of Alfred's cash in Vegas as soon as he could get his huge hands on it. Except for his fantastic body, Jimbo was no different than Daddy had been.

She swerved to avoid an armadillo and nearly lost control of the old Ford. She had better control her nerves if she ever wanted to see Alfred's money. Poor Alfred. Candy took a swig of whiskey.

* * *

Alfred slowed to thirty to gawk at a serious accident, surrounded by fire trucks, cop cars, and ambulances, hovering like buzzards over the carnage. He felt sick when he saw the red stain on the pavement from the flipped sedan. He hoped to God it was coolant or brake fluid. The accident validated his decision to remove all his money from his accounts, leave his wife and children, and run away with Candy. Life was too precious to waste away in a job he didn't like and a marriage he didn't want.

Rebecca had stood by him faithfully these last twenty years. Good reliable, monotone, boring Rebecca, who bore him three boys who except for being the wrong gender, were exactly like their mother. Boring. She knew sixteen years ago their marriage wasn't working, so she got pregnant to keep her and Alfred together. The boys were nothing more than band-aids on a gaping wound. The marriage was a failure.

But now he had another chance and her name was Candy. They had met at the library. He was there for his writing group meeting and her for pottery class. She dropped a beautiful vase in front of him. While picking up the first of the forty-two shards, they struck up a conversation that lasted until the library closed.

One thing led to another and soon they were in his bed. She had been recently jilted by her fiancé and was emotionally spent. She confessed she was a virgin and asked him to be gentle. He was, caressing her as if she were a baby bird.

The tattoo of a butterfly in the small of her back surprised him but she explained her sorority Epsilon Mu Epsilon forced her to get the tattoo with the initials of the sorority emblazoned across the monarch.

Alfred opened the suitcase next to him and stared at the cash. $382,435. Enough to live on in San Diego and travel to Tijuana where Candy could sell her pottery to tourists. He closed the briefcase and thought of sweet Candy.

* * *

Candy forced herself to keep her eyes open. The coke had worn off and it was difficult to read the signs along the highway. She had to be careful not to miss the motel in the hazy dark. Jimbo should be in the room by now, waiting for her and Alfred to walk in, Alfred unaware of Jimbo behind the door waiting with the tire iron.

Why Jimbo always had to use a tire iron on her Johns was a mystery. Maybe it reminded him of his burglary days before his ten year stint in Angola Prison, or maybe he just liked the sound it made when it came crashing down on a skull. Who the hell knew what made Jimbo tick. He was a good partner and always seemed to have an endless supply of drugs.

She felt a little guilty luring Alfred to his demise, or probable demise, depending on how Jimbo felt when he let him have it. Alfred was a nice guy and easily manipulated. Three times in bed with Alfred and she had convinced him to cash out two 401Ks and withdraw everything from checking and savings. Three hundred thousand or something like that, and all in cash.

Poor Alfred believed they would live together in California near the Mexican border and live off the cash while she supplemented their income with pottery sales. What a dope.

She had almost blown it that first time in bed together when he saw her tattoo. Virgins don't normally sport tattoos. She was proud of her quick thinking, telling him her sorority forced the butterfly tat on her and that E.M.E. stood for Epsilon Mu Epsilon. If he had known it was the initials for the Mexican Eagle gangs she used to work for, he would have freaked.

Just a little further to go and Jimbo could whack the little guy and then it's off to Vegas with three hundred glorious grand. Candy blinked her eyes to try to focus. Not far to go but if she could find the damn baggie, she could snort what was left to stay awake.

A large hill loomed ahead on the dark highway. She remembered Jimbo saying the motel wasn't too far after the hill. Still, the coke would help. As the Ford labored up the steep incline, she felt again for the baggie. She spread the last of the lovely powder on her left hand as the car veered slightly over the line. She sniffed deeply and her eyes went wide when she saw the headlights coming toward her.

* * *

Rebecca would be wondering where he was. In twenty years, he had always called when he was late, but not this time. In a short while, he'd be in the arms of his voluptuous Candy, the sweet smell of magnolia or gladiola blossoms everywhere on her. She must add the fragrance to her bathwater.

In a day or two, Rebecca would realize he had emptied their accounts. She gave him the idea right after he met Candy. Rebecca jokingly said she could legally empty their bank accounts and there was nothing he could do to stop her.

"Why's that, dear?" he asked.

"Look at a check, stupid," she said. "It says Alfred or Rebecca Billington, not and. Either one of us can withdraw money without the other's permission."

It was true, and not only the checking account, but the savings and credit unions also.

The teller looked at him funny when he asked for the thousands in cash but it was as Rebecca said, perfectly legal. The 401ks took a few weeks to cash in and there was a hefty penalty for early disbursement, but it still came to a large amount of cash. He and Candy should be able to live for years, and once he had divorced Rebecca, he might even get some cash from the house.

Like he had thought earlier, he wasn't bad, he just did some bad things. Was it worth it? He patted the briefcase full of cash and smiled.

Alfred needed to pee and he wished he had some coffee to wake him up. The monotonous nighttime drive was lulling him to sleep. Just a few more miles and he'd be in her arms and wish he could never leave them.

"Damn!" he said as he realized he had passed the motel. Well, there was nothing he could do about it. He'd have to go over the steep hill ahead and make a u-turn when he could.

Alfred rubbed the briefcase again for comfort and then nearly choked on his spit when he saw the headlights coming toward him.

She'll Be the Death of Him

Driftwood Anthology *Volume XXVIII 2009*

"This introduction may be longer than the actual twisted tale that follows, which should clue the reader on the author's inability to use words of more than two syllables. Vocabulary is not his forte, I'm afraid.

The protagonist of this tale apparently has no name, she an abused and vengeful woman who apparently has had enough of her man.

There is a rather detailed description henceforth of a simple device capable of doing much harm. I recommend you not build it unless of course you've gathered many to observe its purpose. You'll see what I mean. Here's some Good advice—always look up."

~ *G.R.*

She'd had enough of him, the verbal abuse, his infidelity, the beatings. She'd just had enough, and it was stopping as of right now. If her plan worked, not only would the abuse stop, but he'd be gone forever, and—if everything went as planned, she may even get a new house.

She hoped the third time would be the charm as she lit the acetylene torch with the flint striker. The other two light bulbs had been a disaster. Holding the flame on the base too long had melted the glass into a sticky blob.

She carefully held the hundred-watt light bulb in her left hand with an oven mitt, while concentrating the blue flame of the torch on the threaded base. This time, she lifted the flame off the metal base every few seconds until it was just hot enough to separate from the glass bulb. When she heard the air rush in to replace the vacuum from the bulb, she shut off the torch and quickly placed another oven mitt on her right hand. Slowly, she separated the metal base from the glass bulb, making sure not to damage the filament. Then she took the one-gallon can of gasoline off the workbench, filled a plastic cup, and carefully poured it into the light bulb until it was completely full.

With the bulb wrapped in a washcloth to prevent it from breaking, she placed it in a vise on the workbench and slowly screwed the jaws around it to hold it steady. Then she rubbed some epoxy on the narrow end of the bulb and inside the metal base and slipped the two pieces together.

She stared down at the completed project and realized the gasoline bomb represented a future free of his vicious beatings. It also represented her future financial independence, especially if the house burned down and the money started to flow in from the home and life insurance policies.

One step to go and she'd be rid of the bastard forever. All that was left was to screw the gasoline-filled bulb into the socket on the ceiling of the workroom and wait for him to come home. If everything worked properly, he'd come home drunk as usual, walk directly into the workroom, and grab a tall one from the old spare refrigerator in the room used exclusively for beer. Except she knew he'd never get that far, since he had to switch on the overhead light first.

The workroom was the perfect location for her murderous plan. The light switch was three feet from the door, so he would be well into the room's interior by the time he switched on the light. With the switch on, the 120 volts would push less than an amp of current through the filament, but it would be enough to burn it white hot. In a matter of seconds, the filament would reach the correct temperature and ignite the gasoline into an enormous explosion raining fire and glass on him. Soon after his body was aflame, the gas can and propane tanks stored nearby would explode, obliterating the room, the house, and him, thus alleviating her burden forever. Then she'd be free. As if to justify her actions, she felt the bruise on her left cheek, still tender from the previous night's beating.

She made sure the light switch was off before setting the stepladder directly underneath the overhead light. She shined the flashlight on the socket as she screwed the gasoline bomb into it. Just as she had finished screwing it in, she saw his huge shoulders and spiky hair silhouetted in the doorway from the eerie light of the kitchen.

"What the hell are you standing in the dark for?" he asked, as he reached for the light switch.

Oil Man

Honorable Mention Writers Digest *78th Annual Short Story Competition*

Honorable Mention 2010 FFWA Short Story Competition

"How is oil created if not from the carcasses and remains of the dead? A stretch of a segue to lead into the story but with some truth to it.

It is the early 1950s and our hero, Joseph Polansky, a WWII hero, is excited about his new managerial job with Belzer Oil. His euphoria lasts only a year as he is beset with personal and professional issues, his beautiful wife Charlene, foremost on his mind. He suspects, and he rightly should, that she is cheating on him. Not a wise thing to do since Joseph is both the jealous and the vengeful type.

Soon he acquires a gun and a mindset to use it. Will Joseph enact his punishment for this wrong? Will he add to my coffers the lovely Charlene and her lover? Will there be a twist?

What do you think? You bought the book."

~ G.R.

Joseph wrung his large meaty hands repeatedly as Charlene's words bit at his psyche. "I'll never share your bed again as long as you stink like that."

Six years of marriage and a vow of obedience. He'd built her a house, worked ten hours a day, seven days a week to provide for her, to buy expensive things for her, and it meant nothing. To have and to hold until death do us part. That was one vow he'd keep; until death do us part, but she didn't keep her vows and now he'd kill her and all because he smelled like fuel oil.

What did she expect? A man works in harsh conditions all day pumping heating oil so the good citizens of Cleveland can stay warm in the winter, yet she complains he stinks of oil. That's the smell of money. That's the smell of hard work. It should smell like perfume to her and she should thank God for her good fortune, the conniving, thankless, selfish, adulteress. The last thing she'd smell on earth would be the heating oil on his hand as he pulled the trigger.

Adulteress.

"Good evening, Mr. Polansky." Joseph had not expected anyone to speak to him on the bus ride back to his neighborhood from the Belzer Oil office. It was Maddy Olsen, the old biddy, the gossip, always sticking her pig's nose in everyone's business. He had no time, no patience for her today.

"Mrs. Olsen." He gave a polite nod. People rarely sat next to him on the bus. The smell of the oil kept a three-foot barrier between him and the rest. That was the way he liked it. Even after repeated baths, the stink would stay with him. Just ask Charlene. Maddy Olsen must have some very important gossip if she'd risk his gaseous fumes in order to talk to him.

"How is Mrs. Polansky?" she asked, obviously leading up to what she really wanted to talk about. So, the gossip would be about Charlene. He wasn't surprised. He had stayed faithful. There would be no gossip about him.

"Fine," he said curtly. His tone did nothing to dissuade her.

"Oh, wonderful. I remember the last time I saw her. She was downtown, on 25th, I think. Yes, that was it, 25th Street. She drives that cute blue car of yours. It's so nice you let her have the car while you take the bus. Lovely car. Ford, isn't it?"

"Studebaker. She needs it for her job at Wilmington's."

"Oh, yes, quite the modern woman. Oh, how the world's changed in just six years since the war, don't you think?"

"Uh huh." Maybe if he just agreed with everything she said, she'd shut up.

"Yes. Well, anyway, I saw Charlene at that shoe store. What's it called? Mallory's? I forget. She must have bought several pairs of shoes, I imagine."

Here it comes, the big revelation and then his surprised and hurt expression. Well it wasn't going to happen. Poor Maddy would be sorely disappointed. He played along.

"Why's that?"

"Because, she was there several hours. My goodness that's a long time to shop for shoes. You do suppose she was shopping for shoes, don't you?"

Joseph smiled. "No, Maddy, I suppose she was robbing the fucking joint. Now do you mind? I've had a long day."

Maddy stood, sniffed the air, then walked determinedly to mid-bus.

Joseph stared back at his hands. They were large hands. Everything about him was large, his hands, his head, shoulders. Even his nose. All his life they teased him about his size. Schoolmates called him the big dumb Polack.

The name stuck even during the war. Until Anzio, anyway. Three Krauts fired at his division from a high rock emplacement, decimating his platoon. Joseph waited for the orders but none came. Then the dumb Polack charged without regard to his life, headlong into the machine gun nest. He took several rounds before he reached the enemy soldiers. He used his huge hands like sledgehammers to knock two of the enemy out. The third he strangled. He was no longer a big dumb Polack. After that, he was Staff Sergeant Joseph H. Polansky, war hero. His hands had made him a hero. The same hands Charlene fled from the other night.

"Don't you touch me with those ugly things. You make me sick."

The words stung. When he had returned from the war, he was a hero. His old boss at Belzer Oil made him a manager. Girls flocked to Joseph. Pretty girls, beautiful girls. Girls like Charlene gave themselves to him, willingly.

His father warned him. "She's too beautiful, Joseph. She'll break your heart someday. Don't be a fool."

But he was a fool and he is a fool. When he quit the manager's position and went back to his job as an oil pumper, things changed. Charlene no longer bragged about him. The luster of the war hero had worn off. His father's words came back to haunt him. "She's too beautiful."

Joseph reached overhead for the cord. The bus came to a stop.

"You still got two blocks yet, Joe," the bus driver reminded him.

"I'll walk."

When the bus left, Joseph walked into Candle's gun shop. He pointed to a pistol in the glass case. "Give me that .38 and a box of ammo."

"Yes, sir," the proprietor said, and slid the door over to retrieve the weapon. He placed it on the counter. "You know how to use it?"

"I'm a vet. What do you think?"

"Okay, buddy, don't be sore. Just trying to help out. That'll be twenty-five and two—twenty seven altogether."

It was only two blocks to the row house so he only had a short time to rethink his plan. He'd formulated it for over a month now, since he had first found out about Charlene's affair. She was screwing Mitch Brewer, a damn shoe salesman. She could have at least picked someone with a better job, but Joseph knew she picked Brewer because he wasn't an ugly Polack; he was a good-looking shyster. They deserved each other and they would be with each other forever once Joseph blew their brains out. When that was done, he'd blow his own out. Why not? He couldn't think of a reason not to.

He opened the front door with his key and yelled out, "Charlene!" while all the while caressing the gun in his coat pocket. He had decided he'd do it right away with no dramatics. Shoot the lying whore and then go to Brewster's place and do the same to him.

There was no answer. A white sheet of paper hung from the radio. He read Charlene's note. "Went to Mary's for the weekend." Mary was Charlene's sister in Cincinnati.

His anger raged. He needed to do something and soon. He didn't want to wait. He couldn't wait. He decided he'd kill Brewster, take a bus to Cincy, and then kill Charlene and himself. He had to do it now before he changed his mind.

He walked the mile to Brewster's house. The entire time, he made himself think of his humiliation, of how poorly she treated him after all those sacrifices for her.

Joseph waited several seconds after knocking on the front door. He was about to leave when he heard noises from the backyard. He walked around the house to find an attractive woman in a housedress and apron, hanging clothes to dry. It was too damn cold for the outfit and too damn cold to hang clothes.

"Yes?" she asked.

"Is Mr. Brewster in?"

"No. Who are you?" She placed the wet clothes in a basket and removed the apron. Even dressed in her loose clothes, Joseph could see she was beautiful.

"Just a friend. Could you tell him I'd like to see him?"

Arms akimbo, she stared several long, uncomfortable seconds. He fingered the gun.

"I know you. You're Joseph Polansky."

Joseph said nothing and held the gun tighter. He placed his index finger on the trigger.

"Are you here to kill Mitch?" she asked.

The question caught him off guard. He released his tight grip on the revolver.

"You're here to kill Mitch because he's screwing your wife, aren't you?"

Joseph would have to kill her now. What other choice did he have? Soon she'd scream and yell for the police and he would have accomplished nothing.

"My name is Sandra Brewster. I'm Mitch's wife. You're thinking of killing me too, aren't you Joe?

There was no reason to stay quiet anymore. If he had to, he'd shoot her before she called out.

"Charlene is my wife. I know she went along with it, but she's still my wife and he shouldn't be screwing another man's wife. He'll get what he deserves. I don't want to hurt you, so please." Joseph pulled the revolver out of his coat pocket and gestured for her to move out of the way.

Her eyes went wide for a moment and then she returned to a calm demeanor.

"I don't care if you kill him. Your wife isn't the first. I want you to kill him. And then I guess you'll kill Charlene if you haven't already. I really don't care."

"How do you know about Charlene?"

Sandra smirked. "He doesn't hide it. The bastard brags about it. I don't think you've shot Charlene yet anyway."

"How would you know what I've done?"

"Because, she's with Mitch right now at a shoe convention in Atlantic City. She leave you a note?"

Joseph nodded. Now he didn't know what to do. He'd still get them somehow. Bad luck. His whole life seemed to be cursed with bad luck.

"Come inside," Sandra ordered.

At first, Joseph thought he might run away but then followed her up the concrete steps to the kitchen. The warm air felt good.

"Sit down," she said. "Coffee?"

Joseph shook his head and placed the gun back in his coat pocket. Sandra poured some for herself and sat across from him.

"So, Joseph Polansky. I know why Mitch fools around on me. He's the kind of guy that likes variety and wants girls to like him. Narcissistic and vain. How about Charlene? Same thing?"

"Maybe." Joseph said. He stretched his arms out on the table. "Mostly because she doesn't like how my hands smell."

Sandra sniffed. "Smells like gasoline." She picked his hands off the table and leaned over to smell them. "I like the smell. Big hands. I bet you're a real big man, Joseph."

Joseph pulled his hands back. Her eyes sparkled. She was very attractive. Why would Brewster have to go outside his own house for women? He deserved to die.

Sandra sipped her coffee. "I have a favor to ask of you, Joseph."

"What favor?"

"Like I said, I don't care if you kill Mitch. I've wanted to kill him for years, but I have two children. Boy and a girl. One's six and the other's eight. I work fulltime downtown at Benton's as a secretary, but I don't make much money. Mitch does all right at the shoe store, but if you put a bullet in his head my children and I are going to have to live off my salary. You see?"

Joseph nodded.

"But," she continued, "here's the way it is. Today is December fifth. After January first I qualify for the benefits package at Benton's. They'll allow me at that time to get a life insurance policy for Mitch and it will only cost me five dollars a week. You understand?"

Joseph shrugged.

"You're a real man, Joseph, but you're not very bright. If you wait until after the first of the year I'll be able to collect the $20,000 policy on his life. All I'm asking you to do is wait three or four weeks. Please—for my kids. And nobody wants their daddy dead for Christmas even if he deserves it."

She lifted Joseph's hands and kissed them. "Please."

Joseph didn't know what to do. Would this be a way of redeeming himself with God? Would this erase the mortal sins from his soul? He felt a little better. A form of atonement for his sins made him feel better. Yes, he would wait.

"All right."

Sandra cried and kissed Joseph's hands again. The tears dammed up between his fingers. "Thank you, Joseph. Thank you. I'll do anything if you do this." She looked in his eyes. "No one's home. The kids won't be back for a few hours." She rubbed his arm, then stood and walked over next to him. Sandra pressed her hip into his arm. Her leg was soft and warm.

Joseph stood. "I'll keep my vows."

He opened the backdoor.

"Wait. When the policy clears, I'll call you. I'll make sure Mitch is home."

Joseph nodded and walked out.

It took all his patience to wait those agonizing four weeks for Sandra's call. Fortunately, his anger was fortified by Charlene's blatant continuation of her torrid affair with that bastard Brewster. Finally the call came, but it couldn't have come at a worse time. Charlene was again out of town. There was nothing he could do but kill Brewster and then track her down.

Again, he walked to Mitch and Sandra Brewster's house. Sandra informed him on the phone that she and the children would be gone and Mitch would be by himself. The backdoor was unlocked, as Sandra had promised. Joseph heard the radio in the living room. He walked quietly, revolver in hand, hammer locked in the firing position. He'd face Brewster like a man, say nothing, and then kill him. Then it was off to find Charlene.

Brewster was asleep in a recliner, one hand stuck in his underwear and the other held tightly around a can of beer. Joseph shut off the radio.

Brewster's eyes opened. Joseph saw the fear in them as he raised the pistol. Two shots, both in the chest. Brewster squirmed for a few seconds, then slumped over in the chair and stopped breathing. Joseph started to leave when he saw two women standing behind Brewster's death chair.

It was Sandra Brewster and—Charlene. Joseph only managed to say, "Charlene," when Sandra bent down level with her husband's corpse. She held a pistol aimed at Joseph. He instinctively raised his revolver, but it was too late. Sandra fired two shots. The bullets slammed into

Joseph's chest and shoulder. It felt as if someone had smashed him twice with a heavy hammer. He fell into a sitting position, his back against the large radio console.

Joseph touched the warm blood as it oozed out of his wounds. He was confused. He stared up at the women wondering why they had done this horrible thing to him.

Sandra handed her gun to Charlene who wiped it judiciously with a handkerchief and then carefully placed it in Mitch's cold hand. She leaned over and pointed it once again at Joseph, then carefully manipulated Mitch's finger on the trigger.

Joseph jerked as the third bullet hit above his breastbone.

They had killed him, but why?

As light faded, he watched the women embrace in a passionate kiss.

J.J. WHITE

Left Rear Tire

Top Ten Story, 2012 FWA My Wheels Anthology
as chosen by Julie Compton

"Sadly, the death of a child is sometimes inevitable, there being so many around. As I wrote in the fore-word, my employers both above and below, mostly above, wish for the variety of small children to brighten the afterlife.

Bill Pendleton is a man at the nadir of his photo-journalist career, still hoping for that one special photograph that will win him the Pulitzer Prize he desires. When the opportunity arrives, he jumps at the chance. But at what price?"

~ G.R.

Bill Pendleton balanced his donut, coffee, and cigarette, while avoiding snowbirds who impeded his progress toward another humiliating photo assignment. He swerved his '98 Saturn Coupe around an Ontario couple in a Cadillac CTS using just his knees to steer.

"How aboot that?" he said to no one in particular.

He was the Marion Globe's head photographer, a title tainted by the fact that he was their only photographer. Twenty-five years of a less than illustrious career with little to show for it other than a small pension five years from now.

Bill's dreams of heroic assignments for major newspapers disappeared with the advent of the digital age. No one read the papers anymore and every Tom, Dick, and Britney had a cell phone camera so there were no more scoops for a professional photojournalist. Just four months ago, the nation's number one photo traversing all the major media outlets was a shot of a flaming airliner taken by an eight-year-old girl with an IPhone.

Bill flicked his cigarette out the window and answered his cell. Tom the frickin' editor.

"I need you to turn around and head to Stonehaven. 1415 Edgewater. A grandfather backed his truck over a three-year-old."

"C'mon, Tom. I'm a mile from the museum. I'm not gonna turn around and drive thirty miles back."

"Did it sound like a request? Get me photos, the story from the cops, and see if you can shoot the parents or the old man. Could make page one."

"Yeah, I'm sure both subscribers will enjoy reading about it. Listen. Do me a favor. Next time send the other photographer, will ya?"

"Good one, Bill. Now move your ass."

Bill u-turned and floored it. The sooner he finished with the accident the sooner he could make the museum shoot. There was a nice dive nearby there where he could get a burger and a beer.

He arrived at the accident scene in twenty minutes. It was a two-story ranch style, a hundred and eighty grand maybe, but too close to the neighbors for Bill's taste. Two sheriff's green and whites were parked at the curb. The F-150 truck was half in half out of the garage. Bill didn't see the tricycle until he had passed the scene. The blood-stain had spread out beneath the kid's bike and extended down the sloped driveway. Yellow police tape stretched from one side of the garage to the tailgate of the Ford.

Something was different about the scene, the way it set up in his photographer's eye. He instinctively knew he was going to shoot something extraordinary. He had been to similar accidents before. It was an all too familiar scene, the parents not paying attention, whether it was backing a car out of a garage or leaving a pool fence open. But this looked different and he didn't know why.

He shaped his fingers into a frame to see the shot as he walked up to Sergeant Waters. The man had been a cop for as long as Bill had been a photographer.

"What'd ya got, Clete?"

"What's the hell's it look like? You still at the Globe?"

"That's right."

"Little girl. Three year old. The usual. The granddad was heading to the 7-11 for some cigarettes. He thought grandma was watching her and grandma thought he was watching her."

Bill looked over at the truck. The huge, left rear tire had crushed the front end of the tricycle. The old man had stopped quickly but the wheel had rotated a few too many degrees and changed his life forever.

"The body?" Bill asked.

"At the morgue. The parents are in California or on a plane back by now. The old man's inside."

Bill had his notebook out. "Did he say anything?"

Waters shrugged. "Just kept saying he didn't see her, over and over again. He broke down and went into shock. He's resting, but I called the paramedics back to look him over. They'll be here soon."

Bill brought out his digital Nikon. "I'm gonna take a few." There was a bloody blanket on the other side of the truck. Bill pointed to it. "Think I could put that in the shot by the trike?"

"Christ almighty, Pendleton. Just take your pictures and get the hell out of here."

"All right, all right. Just asking."

Bill walked behind the truck to the left of the killer wheel. It was too close of a shot although the blood was clearer at that distance. He backed up to the road and looked through the lens. That was it. The story was there all in one shot. Inside the viewfinder a deputy knelt next to the large wheel and stared dispassionately at the blood stain and the crushed tricycle. Bill had the scene perfect, the truck, the house, and the cop, all framed as if it had been staged. He shot twenty photos in as many seconds. He flipped the camera over to look at one of them. It was hard to see in the harsh sunlight but he knew it was perfect.

Back at the office he pulled them up on his computer monitor.

"Oh God," he said as the photo filled the screen. The picture would be his salvation. It would be his Pulitzer. Once it went out over the wire, the major papers would know who he was. The byline under the bloody scene would say Bill Pendleton. This was it.

The first shot he had taken was the keeper. Not only did it show the crushed tricycle, the pool of blood, the deputy, and the huge truck wheel, it also showed an open kitchen window. There, at a table, the grandfather sat holding his head in his hands while a thin blue vortex of cigarette smoke floated above him. The man's cheek glistened from tears.

The perfect picture. The Pulitzer. A new life for an old photographer.

Bill drummed his fingers and stared at the photo. What was the old man thinking? Was he thinking of the little girl he had played with a few hours earlier, or was he thinking about his son and daughter-in-law as they flew the agonizing twenty-five hundred miles home to bury their daughter?

He drummed his fingers some more and then closed his eyes. After a minute, he called up the other nineteen photos and deleted them. Then he deleted all twenty shots from his camera. Only the prize photo remained on his monitor. He stared for a long time and then clicked on it with his mouse. His editor, Tom Wallace, tapped Bill on the shoulder. Bill pressed the delete key.

"You get the shots?"

Bill shook his head. "Camera broke. Piece of junk."

"Great. How about your cell?"

"Sorry, Tom. I guess I forgot I had it. No shots."

"Damn it. Why do I bother? What was that one you had up on the screen?"

"Oh that? That was some guy's Pulitzer.

J.J. WHITE

The Gambler and the Bum

Published 2009 Helium.com, Storywrite.com

"There is a fine line between prosperity and destitution. That fine line involves money of some sort, or the lack thereof. A quick way to lose your money is a trip to Lost Wages, Nevada, a heartless town that makes its sole purpose to extricate those hard earned wages.

I try to keep close to the city, a milieu known for its high suicide rate. Sadly there is little compensation for the bereaved, the poor soul's money usually on its way up north by the time they bury the sucker.

Aaron Gray has begun his slide, gambling everything, owing a debt that will never be repaid. Though destitute himself, he takes pity on a poor hungry bum, who is undoubtedly insane. Will this charitable act save Aaron's soul and life?

Let's hope not."

∼ G.R.

He wasn't really there. Physically, yes, he satisfied the requirement of matter, having mass, and occupying space, but to the horde of pedestrians shuttling by him, he was invisible.

In any other city in the world a well-dressed man in his thirties, sitting on the curb of a busy intersection, crying, no sobbing, with his head in his hands, would draw at least a modicum of attention. In any other city, but this wasn't any other city, it was Las Vegas. And in Las Vegas, everyone who walked around, sidestepped or bumped into Aaron Gray knew exactly why he sat there on the concrete curb with his feet dangerously close to the melee of cars, buses, and wild taxis. They'd seen it before and they'd see it again, the desperate hopelessness of the gambler at the end of his money, suffering the nadir of his personal and professional life.

It was more sad than disturbing, if anyone had even taken notice. If it had been a different city or even a different time, say 1959 instead of the bleak decade of the '70s, someone might have paused for a moment, stooped down, placed a hand on the grieving man, and offered some help. But on this particular day there would be no help, there would be no pity. The masses of tourists and locals had somewhere to be and just enough time to get there, and besides, they had worries enough of their own.

Aaron lamented his woes as he sat sweating in the relentless Nevada sun. How had it happened so quickly? Just a short time ago, months, or maybe it was days, he was unsure of the time after locking himself endlessly in the timeless casinos, he had begun his slide. At the time, he thought little of his marriage, his children, or the house

He began to wish he could go back in time to the way it was. They were happy and in love. Now Shelly, Todd, the house, maybe even the job, washed away, forever. He wished he'd never come. He could be home where the pungent aroma of lasagna drifted in and out of the rooms of his house. Thursday night lasagna. Or was it Thursday, he wasn't sure. He wished it was, but deep in the black part of his soul dwelled a stronger and deadlier wish that nagged at him relentlessly. That wish overcame all others and compelled him as a slave to his master to find money, somewhere, anywhere, and return to the incandescent den of inequity and try, God yes, try to win it all back. He knew he could if he just had a thousand or five hundred. He just knew he could.

Aaron wiped his nose with his hand and stared at his sleeve, wondering what someone would give him for the suit. It was worth the hundred he paid for it in December. He'd take fifty if they offered. He pulled his wallet out from the jacket pocket, removed ten dollars, and folded and refolded the bill he had saved for dinner at the hotel. But he wasn't going to the hotel, not anymore.

"Give me that, son."

Aaron looked up at the old man standing beside him. He was dressed in an old suit that covered a yellow stained dress shirt left open at the collar. His long hair and thin beard was almost all white except for a few streaks of black in the tip. He stunk of urine and cigarettes and looked as if he had slept in his clothes. Aaron thought it was a tossup on who looked more pathetic, him or the bum.

"What?" Aaron asked.

"That," the old man said, pointing at the folded ten-dollar bill. "Give it to me so I can go to Gail's for some clam chowder and banana nut ice cream. I need it for the chowder."

"Gail's?"

"What's wrong with you? Gail's, down on Center Street. Four blocks from here. I like the chowder and the banana nut ice cream. Good chowder, lots of potatoes. I eat the ice cream first, then the chowder. No drink. You ruin the food if you drink anything with it. Hand me that bill, son. I'm tired of talking."

"Let me tell you something, old man. For the last three months I've been in all the casinos around here, every one of them. I stole my family's savings, mortgaged the house, borrowed $15,000 from my credit union at Trent's Accounting, and even sold my son's insurance policy. I won $40,000 and lost $90,000. This is—."

"She makes good chowder," the old man interrupted. "I eat the ice cream first and then I—"

"You said that. Now, I'm not finished. Somebody's going to listen to me, so it might as well be you. It might be too late tomorrow. I lost everything, my family, my house, my job, everything. Do you understand?"

The old man reached for the bill but Aaron jerked it away.

"This is all I have left, this ten dollar bill. I was going to use it for dinner, but you want to hear something pathetic?"

"You give me that money, son," the old man repeated and wiped his nose with the sleeve of his jacket.

"I asked you if you wanted to hear something pathetic?" Aaron shook the bill at the old man. "I wasn't really going to eat lunch. I was going to go back in the casino and play the slots. I still think I can win the money back and have everything back to the way it was. Now is that pathetic?"

"She closes at two. We can both eat with that money. Give it to me. Give it to me and I'll give you this penny. I'll double the amount every day for thirty days and then I'll pay you. Give me that money, son. I want some of that clam chowder. I put pepper on it to get the taste of the ice cream out of my mouth."

The man shivered and Aaron noticed a puddle of urine by the old man's foot. Aaron stood to avoid the pee creeping close to him. He chuckled, unfolded the bill and held it in front of the old man. The man grabbed for it but Aaron pulled it away, bullying the transient.

"You're going to give me a penny for my ten dollar bill?"

"I said I'd double it, son. For thirty days. What are you, stupid, or something? Give me that money—"

"You'll double it," Aaron said sarcastically. "Okay let's see, if you double the amount each day then—okay, in five days you'll owe me sixteen cents. Wow, how could I pass that up?"

"She closes at two. I want that money. I don't want to hurt you. Give it to me. Sometimes she puts in extra potatoes if you ask."

Aaron laughed when he tried to imagine the old man hurting him. The guy weighed ninety pounds at most and could barely walk, let alone fight.

"Here," he said, holding the bill out. "Take it. I don't need it where I'm going, old man. Go enjoy your chowder and banana ice cream."

"Banana nut."

"Excuse me," Aaron said. "Banana nut. Just like you. Go get your chowder and leave me alone."

The old man pulled twice on the bill snapping it like a fresh towel. He grinned as he flipped it over in his hands. "There's enough here for you too, son. Good chowder. I eat the ice cream first, but I don't drink anything with it."

Aaron rolled his eyes. "No thanks, go—good bye. Tell the world how I helped you. Chisel it on my tombstone. Aaron Gray bought an old man some chowder with his last ten bucks and the old man was so happy he peed on himself."

The old man stuck the ten-dollar bill in his pocket. "I'll pay you in thirty days," he said, and walked away.

Thirty days later, a mysterious well-dressed man walked up to the receptionist seated at her desk on the second floor of the Trent Accounting building. She smiled continuously at the large man until he was near.

"May I help you?" she asked.

"Yes, I'd like you to give this to Mr. Aaron Gray. He works here, I presume."

"Well, no—um, yes, he did work here, but I'm afraid he's not here now."

The blond haired man frowned. "I see. Well, could you leave it on his desk for when he comes back?"

The woman shook her head. "No, sir. You see—um, did you know Mr. Gray very well?"

"No, I've never met the man."

"Yes, well you see, Mr. Gray passed away about a month ago. I'm sorry to have to tell you that. He was a very nice man. The death was sudden and unexpected. Would you like me to refer you to Mrs. Gray?"

"No, that won't be necessary." He pocketed the envelope as he walked toward the elevator.

The man returned to his office located on the eighth floor of the Desert Inn hotel. After he made a few phone calls, he walked down the elaborately decorated hallway and knocked on the penthouse door. He waited the customary thirty seconds before knocking again. A faint voice could be heard from inside.

"Yes?"

"It's me, sir."

The automatic door opened slowly, and he stepped into the make-shift hospital room of his employer.

"Did you deliver the check to Mr. Gray?" the old man with the long white beard asked from his gurney.

"No, sir. Mr. Gray is dead. I made some calls and found out he jumped off the dam a few hours after you met."

"Did he, now? Well, tell me Peter, how much money did I save?"

Peter tore open the envelope and read the amount on the check. "$516,332, sir."

"Wonderful." the old man said. "It's a good day after all, isn't it, Peter. I saved a half a million dollars. It is a good day."

"But, sir, the man's dead."

"Yes. Well, I didn't say it was a good day for him, did I? Now go away and leave me. Tear up the check and tell Maria to bring my ice cream. And tell her, Banana Nut!"

The big man backed out of the open door into the hallway. "Yes, sir," he said, and closed the penthouse door. As he walked back to his office, he ripped the check into small pieces and placed them in his pocket. A small section of the check fell on the hallway carpet. Just legible on the section was his employer's signature, Howard Hughes.

J.J. WHITE

ℭ𝔥𝔢 𝔉𝔬𝔵𝔥𝔬𝔩𝔢

*Finalist at the Santa Barbara Writers Conference
National Competition 2011*

Honorable Mention Writers Digest *78th Annual
Writing Competition*

"Of all the commonplace and shallow stories in this anthology I believe this is my favorite. The tale has a completely despicable protagonist, void of a moral or honest bone in his body. The setting is World War II Europe in a rather cold foxhole, this theme and milieu retreaded from the author's previous tales.

Despite that, I rather like Bennie Calabro, a crook from Chicago thrown into battle through no fault of his own. I had nearly given up on our author until the ending woke me. Try to stay awake. It's worth it."

~ *G.R.*

December 23, 1944 – West of St. Vith, Belgium

Private Bennie Calabro, 106th U.S. Infantry, serial number 302478911, was a deserter. He was two miles behind enemy lines, had been bombarded relentlessly by kraut 88s, and was directly in line with the sixth SS Panzer Army's Blitzkrieg as it raced toward Antwerp.

It was dusk when the 106th pulled out and headed east to defend St. Vith. Bennie lagged behind until his division was far enough ahead so that they wouldn't miss him. He hid in hedgerows along the roads and worked his way back to the foxhole where he had spent the last three days.

He knew he still had a good chance of dying, but it wouldn't be by getting his ass shot up charging head on into the Nazi Army like the rest of those idiots.

He was thirty years old, for Christ's sake. He shouldn't have even been out here with a bunch of teenagers stopping rounds with their bodies to protect mom and dad back home. The brass promised them the Germans had all but given up and they'd only have to mop up the stragglers. That was before the whole fucking Kraut Army decided the war wasn't over yet.

Bennie rubbed his hands over the makeshift fire he had built in the large foxhole. The crater had been formed by an artillery shell blast and could easily hold four GI's. The heat from the fire felt good on his hands, but the cold left little sensation in his feet. They weren't supposed to be out in the open when the winter hit. The war was supposed to be over by now. Patton and Montgomery should be splitting Germany with the Commies, and Bennie Calabro was supposed to be heading back to Chicago.

He lay flat on the ground and pulled his helmet down hard over his head when he heard the whistle of a descending artillery round. His body bounced slightly off the ground from the concussion of the nearby shell.

When he sat up to brush off the dirt, he flinched, startled by the soldier sitting against the opposite bank of the foxhole.

"Christ!" Bennie exclaimed. "Where the hell did you come from?"

The corporal didn't answer. He stared ahead, the shadows from the fire dancing across his face, framed by the white smoke.

"You with the 106?" Bennie asked, worried they had sent someone back for him. The soldier stayed silent, his blank stare fixed into space. "You hurt, corporal?"

"No," the young soldier answered.

Bennie figured he was about nineteen. He had the same vacant look as all the other dogfaces coming back from the fight on the front lines. Kids who had killed their first enemy soldier. Damn fools thought it would be all flag waving and glory. Well that was all bullshit. It was blood, death, frozen hands, and frozen feet, and that's all it was. Glory was for generals in their headquarters at Versailles, not for the GIs in their bombed out shit holes surrounded by SS troops.

"What's your name?" Bennie asked, hoping a conversation would relieve the boredom in the silence between the shelling.

Nothing.

The kid was either shell-shocked or just fucking nuts, Bennie thought, as he took two cigarettes out of the pack in his jacket, lit them, and handed one to the corporal. To his delight, the corporal enthusiastically smoked it to a nub.

"Where you from?" Bennie asked.

"Iowa."

That's better, Bennie thought. At least now they had something to talk about. They'd both been in Iowa. Not exactly Chicago, but the conversation would take his mind off his feet.

"I've been to Iowa," Bennie said. "Not that I really wanted to go there, but I had a little trouble in Chicago and thought I'd better leave town for a while until things settled down."

Bennie couldn't tell if the corporal heard a word of what he said, but what the hell; he felt better just having someone to talk to. "That's one of the reasons I'm here. I get in a lot of trouble. Hey, you gotta make a living, you know what I mean?"

The corporal continued his unblinking stare as he held his gloved hands over the fire. A light snow began to fall.

"The judge gave me two choices," Bennie continued. "Go to prison or join the Army. Some choice, huh? What'd the dope think I was going to say, send me to prison, I like it there? Anyway, I figured the war would be over by the time I got over here. Boy, was I in for a surprise. Two days on Omaha Beach getting my ass shot off and now beautiful Belgium. I'm one lucky Joe, huh buddy? Hey, you don't' talk much, do you?"

The corporal cringed at an explosion in the distance.

"Hey, don't worry about them, Corp. If you can hear 'em go off, you're okay. It's the ones you don't hear that kill you."

Bennie lit another Lucky Strike.

"I was telling you about the time I spent there. It was a good time too, I tell you. Virginia Wilson, oh, what a broad. It was in '38 and like I said, I had to hightail it out of Chicago. I was hitching rides outside of Iowa City when some sap dropped me off in a hick town called West Liberty. You ever heard of it?"

No answer from the kid, so Bennie kept going. "Real hick town, but I didn't have no money anyway, except for ten bucks I kept in my hat for emergencies. Anyway, I needed some food and some way to get some bucks to pay for the trip to California. I figured

I could make some dough out West. Lots of broads with money out there.

"Now listen to this. I go inside this dive to order a java and some toast and I get waited on by this gorgeous doll. She looked like one of those Norwegian broads up in Minnesota. A real Jean Harlow type, and oh, she had a nice set of tits, I tell you.

"Well, she and I hit it off pretty good. I gave her this bullshit story about being a big shot back in Chicago and how my car broke down and was getting fixed at the local garage. She fell for it like crazy. We talked for a couple of hours. She had the usual story about her parents running her life and how she wanted out of Hicksville to see the big city. You know the usual bullshit you hear from these country broads. You know what I'm saying?

"Well one thing led to another and before I knew it, we were up in her apartment and our clothes were in a pile by the bed. Virginia Wilson—man oh man she had a set of tits on her. What I wouldn't give to have them wrapped around my face right now. Man oh man.

"Anyway, turns out she's got five hundred bucks saved up and wants to tag along with me back to Chicago after my Caddy gets fixed the next day. Let me tell you something, it was manna from heaven. How could one guy get so damn lucky when it seemed like everything was going to the dogs.

"Next day, she gets the five hundred and starts packing. I talk her into going to the garage across the street and paying for my car repairs. I give her the ten bucks in my hat. I used some excuse like I had to make some collect calls to Chicago or something.

"Here's where it gets good. You still with me kid? Yeah, sure you are. So anyways, while she's across the street, I grab the five hundred out of her suitcase, jump in her jalopy and head West. Let me tell you buddy, Iowa brings up memories for this GI, fond memories. I had me the time of my life on that broad's money. Hell, I even sold the car for two hundred, later. Best damn time of my life.

"You know, every once in a while I think about old Virginia Wilson. I wonder what ever happened to her."

The corporal grabbed his M1 off the wet ground and stood, the glow of the dying fire illuminating his hard face. He aimed the barrel at Bennie and fired one round into a spot just above Bennie's left eyebrow. Bennie's helmet flew off in a spray of brain matter and blood. Bennie slumped over, his head remarkably settling in his own helmet, which quickly filled with blood oozing from the wound.

The corporal stared down at Bennie's corpse. He spoke in a low monotone. "I'll tell you what happened to Virginia Wilson, private. She died giving birth to my nephew."

The Abduction of Laura

Published in Literary Liftoff *Volume 3, Number 2, 2007*

"OMG, as my teenage son would say, despite the years of formal training he underwent to take my place once I retire to Florida. Ah, Florida. Where retirees go to die. I expect it will be a pleasant experience, seeing my son so often.

Anyways. Another word the boy overuses. Why do they call the abduction of an adult a kidnapping when it's obvious there is no kid or napping? I ask you since I gauge your intelligence quota slightly higher than the author's.

No one dies in this tale. Yes, I know, in the foreword I said someone dies in every story, but at the time I didn't realize the author was an idiot and a liar. So sue me, or better yet, threaten me. See what that gets you.

Back to Laura. She's upset at the Space Program, or what's left of it, though once abducted, she puts her life in perspective. The twist in this story is irony. Yes, I know, what can I say, I only introduce the damn things."

~ G.R.

Laura Myers loved her early morning jogs. She loved the routine: waking early, showering, eating a light breakfast and jogging four miles down the road and back before dawn. There was very little traffic out that early, so usually, she jogged on the road. The cool air and the rhythmic beat of her tennis shoes on the asphalt comforted her. Today, she needed all the comfort she could get. Two weeks ago, her husband Bill broke the horrible news that when this last Space Shuttle mission was completed, his company, ISA, planned to lay him off. If that wasn't

bad enough, they also told him that since he only had nineteen years with the company instead of the twenty needed for retirement he won't be receiving a pension or benefits.

Endeavour, Houston. MCC 'go' for deorbit burn.

Roger, Houston go for deorbit burn.

Bill handled the news better than Laura. Laura was angry. She was angry at NASA, angry at ISA, angry at everything associated with the space program.

The day of the launch she went to her church and prayed for God to destroy the Shuttle. She wanted the people who destroyed her life to lose their jobs. Let them see what it feels like. When her prayers failed, and the Shuttle launched, she returned to church and prayed for the mission to fail. Now, as she ran through the darkness, the Shuttle was scheduled to land in one hour. She prayed again to God. She prayed the Shuttle would crash on re-entry.

Endeavour, Houston. MS seat ingress, single APU start.

Roger, Houston. Single APU start. Houston? ETA 07:22 hours?

Roger, Endeavour.

She heard a familiar noise behind her on the road. She had heard it many times before during her runs. It was the sound a car makes when driving over a speed bump. Instinctively, she moved off the road and onto the grass. A slight wind hit her as the car passed. The guy was an idiot to drive with the lights off.

The brake lights blinked on and off a hundred feet in front of her. He must have turned off onto the causeway road. The causeway was her checkpoint for turning back home. She stopped at the intersection and stooped over to catch her breath before continuing the run home.

When she turned to head back, a large man grabbed her from behind. He held a knife to her neck, cupped her mouth with his left hand and dragged her backward toward his car. Laura screamed into his hand and twisted her body trying to free herself from his grip. He made a superficial cut with the knife just below her cheekbone. The warm blood trickled down the side of her face and onto her neck.

"Shut up," the man said in a calm, even voice. "I'll cut you more if you try to scream." Laura bit his hand and kicked his leg. He cut her again, as promised, this time on her chin. She screamed from the intense pain.

"I won't kill you, lady, if you don't fight me," he whispered in her ear. He placed the blade directly under her nose. "Are you gonna shut up?" Laura nodded. "That's better. Now put your head on the seat and don't move, if you want to live."

Endeavour – 21 degree right roll command.

Roger, Houston. 21 degree right roll.

He shoved her face down on the back seat of the car, grabbed her arms, and crossed them behind her back. He used plastic tie wraps to bind her hands and feet.

"Please let me go," she said.

"I don't think so." He flipped her over and placed a strip of duct tape over her mouth. She stared at the huge bearded man. His clothes were dirty, grease stains on his shirt reflecting the interior light of the car.

She screamed into the tape, though the sound was barely audible.

"Yell all you want, sweetheart." He grabbed a large black trash bag and slid it over her feet up to her neck. He pushed her down between the seats, started the car and then drove on to the causeway.

Laura cried when she thought how worried Bill and the girls would be when they realized she was missing. Bill would drive up and down her route trying to find her before calling the police. She regretted crying almost immediately when the tears seeped into her wounds causing more pain. She rubbed her face on the carpeted floorboard trying to wipe the tears out of her cuts.

Endeavour. 51 degree roll reversal.

Roger, 51 degree roll reversal.

"We're gonna go for a little ride, sweetheart. You can be my girl-friend. We've got about ten miles to my secret place. I'll let you know when we're close. It's just a little side road off the Beeline. Be there in no time. No time at all."

Laura thought about earlier in the day when she asked God to destroy the Shuttle. Bill losing his job seemed trivial now that she was going to lose her life.

As the car turned off I-95 and on to the Beeline, it bounced over a bump in the road caused by some uneven pavement. A brown wooden box on the back seat fell down near her head. When it opened, scissors, scalpels, and hemostats fell out on the floor.

"Oh, that's just my toolbox. I'll show it to you in a little while."

The darkness of the early morning gave way to the morning light. Laura looked out the back window of the car and saw the sun rising slightly above the glass. They were heading west. How long till he stops and kills her? She was drenched in her own sweat from the plastic bag. The sweat turned out to be a blessing as she was able to free her hands from the wet plastic binding. She reached up to the door and pulled the door handle. It wouldn't open.

Endeavour? Houston. What's your velocity reading?

Nominal, Houston. Just over Mach 1.

Roger, Endeavour.

She felt for the buttons on the armrest, trying to find the one for the electric door lock. She located the button, but knew if she operated it he would hear the noise. She decided to wait until he slowed the car before opening the door and then she'd pull herself out, knowing it would only be possible when he turned off the highway. She loosened the bag around her neck to allow some air in to cool her body.

"We're almost there. Just a mile—" Before he could finish the sentence there were two terrific explosions, one immediately after the other. The car jerked to the left from the pressure wave.

"Jesus Christ! What the hell was that?"

Several cars in front and behind pulled into the emergency lane.

"I better see what hit us, sweetheart. Don't go anywhere. I'll be right back."

The man exited the car and walked around it looking for damage. He noticed the other drivers in front of him doing the same.

"There's nothing wrong with your car, young man," an elderly man said from behind.

"Huh?"

"It was the sonic booms from the Shuttle landing," the old man said as he pointed to the sky in the east.

"No kidding. Well I'll be damned. Hey, thanks man." The large man returned to his car and started the engine. "Space Shuttle," he said. "Can you beat that?"

Houston, Endeavour on the HAC.

Roger, Endeavour.

Laura reached up and unlocked the door as the man accelerated out of the emergency lane. She pulled the handle and shoved open the door. With her free hand she grabbed the door frame and tumbled out into the highway, screaming into the duct tape as the left rear tire rolled over her foot.

The old man behind them saw the black bag fall out of the car onto the edge of the emergency lane. The car continued accelerating as the rear door flew open wider.

"Hey! Young man! Stop! Young man!" The old man looked down at the black bag and gasped when he saw Laura's hair sticking out.

The car backed up near the black bag. As the old man walked towards Laura and the car, the backup lights went out. The kidnapper reached behind the seat and slammed shut the back door. The car sped off into the traffic.

"Are you all right dear?" Laura nodded. He pulled the tape off her mouth. She gasped for air.

"It's all right now. My wife will call the police and the ambulance. They'll catch him. Here, let's get that bag off you." Other cars stopped nearby and the drivers ran towards Laura and the old man as he pulled the garbage bag off her.

"You're a very lucky girl. You'll have to thank God your prayers were answered."

Laura looked up at the man and whispered hoarsely. "Thank God they weren't. . . .Thank God they weren't."

SLF, Endeavour. Touchdown 07:23 hours.

Roger, Endeavour. Welcome home.

J.J. WHITE

The Writer

First Place Short Story, 2008 Royal Palm Literary Awards
Published in Literary Liftoff, *Volume 3, Number 1, 2006*

"What drives those to write prose, to tell a story that floats in the deepest depths of their psyche, memorable prose, hard hitting emotional prose that entertains, while asking important questions of the reader? Our author obviously has no idea or he'd be writing it instead of this pabulum.

That aside, our nameless protagonist in this aptly titled story, is a writer of sorts. Each day he follows a routine that few could mimic, writing what is in his head on to a full notebook.

A shoe salesman nearby watches this strange man, and wonders what the author writes each day. No, he doesn't just wonder, he obsesses with what the man is writing and won't rest until he finds out.

Is he dying to know? Perhaps. Someone has to die, but you know that."

~ G.R.

I'd sit on the cushioned stool behind the counter and hide my textbooks out of the view of customers. The outside of the counter had large mirrors that let customers admire the shoes they were trying to decide whether or not to buy. These mirrored counters were standard décor for the shoe stores located inside shopping malls throughout the 1970s. The men's shoe store, where I worked, was considered upscale even for a mall. We sold mostly Florsheim and Bally shoes. The after school job helped pay for my college expenses. I worked the hours of four to nine and most of that time I spent studying. Usually there were few customers in our part of the mall during the evening hours.

I first noticed the Writer on one of those quiet nights in the mall. I had yet to wait on my first customer and it was only my second day on the job. My school textbooks covered the big counter. Fred, my co-worker, watched the floor so I could concentrate on my engineering problems.

About 4:30, the Writer walked in the entrance near the J.C. Penney's and sat down on the wooden bench in front of our store. I guessed his age to be early fifties. He dressed in a rustic, multicolored, long-sleeved shirt and light brown khaki pants that had large zippered pockets everywhere. He wore his shirt untucked to hide the forty or fifty extra pounds he was carrying. His full head of dirty brown hair, small beard and mustache gave him that ubiquitous professor look so popular with middle aged men of the time.

The Writer unzipped one pocket on the left side of his pants and brought out some reading glasses, which made him look ten years older. Then he unzipped a right hand pocket to retrieve a pack of unfiltered Camels, a lighter, and an ashtray. He placed the ashtray, cigarettes, and lighter carefully on the bench, then took a notebook from under his arm, placed it on his lap, opened it to the first page, and then pulled several pencils out of the many-pocketed pants. He lit a Camel, smoked for about a minute, and then put the cigarette on the ashtray.

Then he started writing. And writing. And writing. He continued writing until 8:45. At exactly that time, he got up, emptied his ashtray in the trashcan, put the ashtray, pencils, glasses, lighter and cigarettes in his pockets, tucked the now full notebook under his arm and walked out the Penney's entrance. I thought this seemed a little unusual, but no one else seemed to notice.

However, the next day he came back and went through the same routine. He arrived at 4:30 and left at 8:45. The routine was exactly the same, the cigarettes, the ashtray, the glasses, and the pencils. The notebook was identical to the one he had the previous day, except it was blank.

This time I paid more attention to his routine. I noticed a few idiosyncrasies I had missed the night before. At 7:30 he got up from the bench, stretched his arms, and walked over to the ice cream kiosk diagonally across the hall from our store, where he ordered a vanilla ice cream cone, sat at one of the tables and ate the ice cream. At 7:40, he wiped his face, threw away the napkins, and walked back to the bench where he continued to write until 8:45.

The man never varied from this routine. From the pencils, to the writing, to throwing away the napkins, it was always the same. He followed the same exact routine, Monday through Saturday, never faltering, ever diligent, always the same.

The mall was open on Sunday, but I assumed he took that particular day off because he was a religious man or perhaps because the mall closed at six, it threw off his routine. Otherwise, he was there, faithfully writing until a quarter of nine.

But, what exactly was he writing? I estimated he wrote over a hundred pages a day, for the two years that I worked at that store. It's possible he was writing several books. Maybe he was a technical writer, but I never saw him use notes or reference books. He just thought and wrote; and thought some more and wrote some more.

Fred wasn't much help when it came to solving this mystery. I asked him questions about our mall mystery writer, but he knew very little about him.

"The girl over at the jewelry store said he's been coming in for at least four years," Fred said. "No one knows his name or what he's writing about. Mall security leaves him alone as long as he doesn't cause any problems or bother the customers."

After watching him for a week, I decided to try to learn more about him, or at least try to figure out what he was writing. One night he sat on the bench with his back facing our shop. I asked Fred to keep an eye on the floor. I told him I was going to see if I could sneak a look at what the guy was writing. Fred laughed.

"This I gotta see," Fred said. "I can guarantee you won't be able to see much. I know. I've tried before and the guy's too quick."

"Yeah, but I'm not even going to let him see me," I said. "Watch." I stepped out of the store and casually walked up behind the man. As I looked over his right shoulder, he shifted his body to block my view of the notebook. I moved quickly into position over his left shoulder for a better look. He shifted again. Frustrated, I turned back to see Fred grinning at me.

All right, fine then. I'll take the offensive.

I walked to the side of the bench and sat next to him. I was about to start a conversation when he stood and moved to another empty bench. I could hear Fred's laughter behind me.

I found out in subsequent days that this was the Writer's routine. If someone sat next to him, he got up and moved to another bench until his bench was empty and available again. As time went by, it dwelled on me.

Weeks and weeks of his endless writing, chain smoking, and ice creams turned into months and then years. Two years of endless curiosity about this writing machine. Was there a world-renowned author sitting at our bench? Who knew? No one even knew his name. Surely, at least, he was a genius to be able to write so much material and never use references or notes.

Sometimes in the middle of writing, he would pause as if he had a problem with a sentence or paragraph. But then he'd raise his pencil in the air or clap the side of his head as if to say "Eureka," and then get right back to his marathon writing, successfully solving whatever literary problem had faced him.

Two years I suffered, wanting desperately to know more about him. I was obsessed. I wanted to know if he was married, or if he had children. Was he a published author? Was he writing about the Civil War or World War II? Did he eat anything besides vanilla ice cream? (The large belly indicated he did). But the thing I really wanted to know was, why was he there? What made someone spend that much time doing one thing?

One Friday night, the routine changed. The traffic was light in the mall and the Writer arrived at 4:30 just like every other Friday night for the last two years. He had the notebook on his lap and the Camels were next to the ashtray. At 7:30, he ate his ice cream and at 7:40, he continued writing.

At about 8:30 I was helping a customer with some shoes when something out of the corner of my eye caught my attention. The Writer stood. Not particularly unusual if it were 8:45, but it was 8:30. It was much too early for him to leave, and no one had sat down next to him on the bench. I placed the shoes down and stood to look over at him. He turned slightly to his right and looked directly into my eyes. His eyes were bright blue. For two years, I realized, I had never seen the color of his eyes. It occurred to me that he was probably a very handsome man in his youth.

He dropped the notebook, and grabbed his left arm with his right hand. He grimaced in obvious pain. The knees buckled, and he seemed to fall in slow motion to the floor. As his knees touched, he grabbed his chest with both hands, fell forward to the floor—and died.

I ran out of the shop over to the bench. Several customers and employees of other shops walked or ran to surround him in a half circle. I turned him over on his back and listened for his breathing.

A woman said grimly, "Oh the poor man".

A man behind said, "He's dead, just look at his lips." The lips were light blue.

"Did someone call an ambulance?" I asked.

"Yes. Cyndi's calling over at the jewelry store now," someone said.

Security arrived soon after and ordered everyone to just "Move along please." I walked back to my shop, and when I turned back to look at the commotion, several more security guards surrounded the body.

It was then I noticed the Writer's notebook underneath the bench. I nonchalantly walked out of the shop and picked it up. The security guards were too busy to notice me. I'm sure if they had, they would have asked for it. I thought about offering it to them, but the two years of obsessive curiosity about the notebook's contents prevented me. I put the notebook near my chest and covered it with my arms, shielding it from Fred, customers, and security guards. I walked over to the mirrored counter and hid the book under the shelf.

Finally, I was going to see what he had been writing in those notebooks for all those years, for all those endless hours. My heart raced and my hands shook in anticipation. I opened the notebook to a middle page. I stared at it, awestruck.

There were three sentences on each line. The same three sentences, over and over again on every line of the page. I flipped through the pages. Each was identical to the previous one. Every notebook he had filled over the years must have been—identical.

Stunned. Almost in shock, I read the lines again.

I miss you, Mary. I'm sorry. Please come back.

Gathering FDR's Spirit

"FDR is dead, but did you know that his spirit lives on near his tombstone in Hyde Park? Neither did I and I still remember wheeling the naïve patrician, who abandoned his aristocratic lifestyle to serve the public, on to his eternal resting place.

Evidently I was mistaken about shuttling the president to his maker as our author now has the protagonist, Kesegowaase, a Penobscot Indian, supposedly gathering Roosevelt's soul into him. So what do I know? I'm only Death.

Although FDR is technically dead he is not the dead man this story revolves around. Instead, it dwells on a man who committed a heinous crime many years ago and must now pay his penance.

My question is, will someone gather his soul someday?"

~ G.R.

That was something you didn't see every day, two Indians, wrapped in colorful blankets, sitting in the middle of Route 2. Officer Ray Willard winced as cars slowed to avoid the old men who seemed not to notice or care about the danger. He flipped on the lights and siren as he approached the men at full speed. He'd seen a few Indians drunk on their asses in the area a few years back in '49, but not as old as these boys. He called it in.

"103, dispatch."

"103."

"Need some help on Route 2 about a mile north of town. Signal thirty-nine.

"114 is the closest, Ray. What's going on?"

"I've got two Indians sitting in the middle of the road. Need a car to slow traffic behind me."

"They Penobscot, from the island?"

"No, Maggie, they're from Bombay. Where the hell else would they be from?"

"Okay, Okay. Stand by."

Ray got out of the cruiser, unsnapped his holster, and stood in front of the Indians. Both had long gray hair and bright red headbands and either one could have been the model for the nickel. The one on the left sat cross-legged and head down as if he were watching ants crawl across his boots. They'd be from Indian Island, about three miles from there. The one on the right lifted his head.

"Are you Windego?" he asked.

"Who?"

"The great demon."

"You want to tell me what you two think you're doing sitting the middle of the damn road?"

"So, I'm not dead? I was hoping I was dead. We should not have come here. Askuwheteau is stupid, but he is my brother-in-law so I listen to him out of respect for my dead sister."

The old Indian on the left looked asleep. Ray nudged him with his foot, but the old coot kept his head down. His blanket jutted out a few inches from behind him like he was a hunchback or something. Ray turned back to the talkative one.

"What's wrong with his back?"

"He has a knife sticking out of it."

Ray pulled aside the blanket. A huge hunting knife protruded from the back of the old man. It had been shoved in nearly to the hilt. Ray pulled his revolver and pointed it at Indian number two.

"You kill the man?"

"No, he killed himself."

"Killed himself. Stabbed himself in the back with the knife."

"Yes," the Indian said. He was very flexible."

"Okay, Chief. Get up and put your hands behind your back. Your brother-in-law upset you or something? That why you did it?"

Ray clicked the handcuffs on him. As the old Indian ducked his head to sit in the backseat, he said, "My sister could have chosen better."

* * *

Attorney Socalexis Dana twisted around in his seat to scan a court-room full of interested Milford townsfolk. A packed house. Normally a trial involving Indians got little publicity, but his client attracted plenty with the claim that his brother-in-law, Jessie Francis, had committed suicide by stabbing himself in the back.

No one believed John Orono, who insisted on using his Indian name, Kesegowaase. Socalexis had defended a few members of the tribe in this courtroom and though many of the Penobscot fought in the recent war, there was still a good amount of prejudice passed down the generations from the first time a white man shoved a Maine Indian from his home.

Kesegowaase had done well on the stand so far, but the District Attorney Maxwell Hardy, was a tough and experienced prosecutor who would rip the incredulous story apart. Hardy paced in front of the old Indian.

"Mr. Orono. Tell the court again, this time in detail. Starting from the time you left the reservation until the death of Mr. Francis on Route 2."

The Indian said nothing.

"Mr. Orono?"

"My name is Kesegowaase."

"Your birth certificate says you are John Orono."

"That is my white-man name."

"Fine, Kesego—"

"Kesegowaase.

"Your story."

"There is not much to tell. Askuwheteau and I didn't want to die on the island—"

"By Askuwheteau, you mean Jessie Francis, your brother-in-law?"

"Yes. We were old men and the young men on the island didn't want us around so I said we should go somewhere to gather spirit and die."

"Gather spirit?"

"Yes. I wanted to gather Franklin Roosevelt's in New York and my brother-in-law wanted to gather John Wilkes Booth's because he hated Lincoln for some reason. Askuwheteau was stupid."

"So you went to New York."

"Yes. To Hyde Park. To gather Roosevelt's spirit from his grave."

"You don't really believe that do you?"

"I accepted his spirit that day, but John Wilkes Booth's grave is in Baltimore and we didn't want to take a bus there."

"So you have Roosevelt's spirit in you now?"

"Yes. He never stops talking. He is always complaining like a woman about President Truman and other things I know nothing about. I had thought if I took his spirit, I could also be a great man. I regret my decision."

The district attorney shook his head. "And why did you and your brother-in-law end up in the middle of Route 2?"

"We thought someone would run us over. I wanted to die because no one wanted me anymore."

"And your brother-in-law?"

"He wouldn't tell me, but he said it was for something he did in the past."

"And by some remarkable feat of agility he stabbed himself in the back."

"He was very flexible."

"I think we've heard enough of your nonsense."

Socalexis objected, but the judge overruled. The jurors seemed to shake their heads in unison, as if they all thought the Indian crazy.

Hardy continued.

"Could you tell the jury who Mary Orono was?"

"She was my sister."

"And she was married to Jessie Francis—your brother-in-law?"

"Yes."

The attorney held up a paper.

"I have state's evidence number four here, a death certificate for Mrs. Mary Orono Francis, dated December 12, 1910. It says she died from blows to her head and body. The tribal police report at the time, state's evidence number five, says her husband, Jesse Francis, was a suspect but was never arrested. That's why you stabbed your brother-in-law, to avenge your sister's death, a death you blamed on Mr. Francis You've had to live with the knowledge that this man killed your sister forty years ago and got away with it. So you sat on that highway and waited until there was no traffic and then you shoved that knife in him to finally pay him back for taking away your sister from you. Didn't you?"

The old Indian looked straight ahead.

"She was a good sister."

* * *

The jury deliberated for one hour. The head juror handed the note to the judge who read it aloud.

"We the jury, find the defendant, John Orono, not guilty."

Socalexis turned and shook the old Indian's hand.

"Congratulations, Kesegowaase. I'm surprised they believed you."

The old man nodded.

"I think they realized there are some very flexible people in the world."

J.J. WHITE

Miguel

First Place Flash Fiction, 2007 Royal Palm Literary Awards
Proteus Review, *Volume 4, Number 1, 2006*

"There are so many stories lately dealing with Mexican drug cartels, one would think no legitimate author would beat that dead horse one more time. One would think.

Apparently our author believes the reading public enjoys stereotypical characters engaged in gratuitous violence that results in senseless deaths. I must admit, it has potential.

Thankfully the story is gloriously short."

~ G.R.

Miguel opened the door to the cantina. The room smelled like marijuana and stale beer. When his eyes adjusted to the light, he saw many men sitting on one side of a large wooden table. These men were all trying to get the attention of their boss, who sat in the middle of the table. The scene reminded Miguel of Da Vinci's Last Supper. The boss was a skinny gringo with long dirty blond hair and a thin brown mustache. A green baseball hat blocked his eyes when he tipped his head. On the table in front of the man, lay a suitcase and a machine gun. The men sitting around him looked up to eye Miguel. Each man had a small shotgun and a pistol in front of him.

"*Buenos dias, Miguel,*" the grimy man in the green hat said, waving a slow burning joint in the air for emphasis. "I think we've got a little problem here, amigo. I see $40,000 worth of cash in this suitcase of mine, and you only delivered half the coke I asked for. I'm guessing you're either here to give me the rest of my coke or maybe you're just here to explain where it is."

Miguel felt inside his shirt for the Uzi. He was about to remove it, when his woman walked in the door. Maria walked over to Miguel, ignoring the catcalls of the men at the table, and placed her hand on his shoulder. Maria was so beautiful, her face angelic, her breasts soft and full. Miguel was proud that that the most beautiful girl in town belonged to him.

"Miguel," she said softly. "Come away from here. These men are dangerous. I do not want you to get hurt over this. Please?"

Miguel shifted his eyes off the gringo, grabbed Maria's head, pulled her down, and kissed her passionately.

"Maria, go outside and wait for me while I deal with this scum." He pushed her away and she rushed out of the cantina.

"Well," said the gringo in the green hat. "I guess from the way you're acting, that you don't have the rest of my coke."

"That is correct, senor," Miguel said, pulling the Uzi out of his shirt.

Miguel sprayed the bullets across the table, killing the five men to the left of the gringo. The other men grabbed their guns and fired back at Miguel, the bullets ricocheting around him. He dove under the bench, grabbed two of the men by their feet, and pulled them under the table. He stabbed both of them in the heart with his switchblade. The four remaining men fired their guns at him, but the table he had pushed over blocked the bullets. His Uzi empty, he slammed his foot down on one of the dead men's automatic weapon. As it flipped in the air, Miguel caught it with his left hand. He shot toward the four remaining men, their bodies jumping as the bullets riddled their torsos.

Now it was just the gringo and him. He aimed the gun at the man in the green hat and pulled the trigger, but the weapon was empty. The gringo laughed at Miguel and raised his pistol. He fired, but the bullet only grazed the Mexican's head. He pulled the trigger again, but this time the gun jammed. He threw down the weapon, faced Miguel, and went into a karate stance.

"Just you and me, Mexican, mano-a-mano," the gringo said, "and just so you'll know ahead of time, I'm the black belt champion of Dallas, Texas."

Miguel threw down the gun and raised his fists. The gringo jumped over the table, his blonde hair bouncing wildly beneath his hat. He stepped over a dead body and whipped his legs into the air toward Miguel's head. Miguel feinted left, avoiding the blow. He swung his arm in an uppercut, breaking the gringo's chin. The gringo fell to the floor, unconscious, as Miguel grabbed an automatic weapon from one of the dead men. He aimed it at the gringo in the green baseball hat, and fired at the motionless body.

"You may be the karate champion of Dallas, gringo, but I am the boxing champion of Guadalajara." He threw down the gun, grabbed the suitcase of money, and walked out of the cantina. Outside, in the doorway, stood Maria.

"*Gracias a Dios, esta's bien,*" she said, hugging Miguel. "Did you kill them all?"

"Yes, Maria," Miguel replied. "They are all dead."

"Oh, Miguel," she said breathlessly, brushing her large breasts against his arm. "I get so excited when I see you fight. Take me to my room and make love to me for hours."

Maria placed a hand on Miguel's arm, and with her other hand, she tapped him on the side of his head. Then she tapped him again and again.

"Miguel? Hey amigo, get up!" the man said, tapping Miguel with his hammer." We got two more roofs to shingle. Get your Mexican ass up! Siesta is over."

Miguel wiped the sleep from his eyes and lifted himself up from the side of the house where he had been leaning. He strapped on his tool belt and grudgingly followed the foreman back to the building that they had been working on.

"Come on amigo, we ain't got all day," said the foreman who had long dirty blond hair and wore a green baseball hat.

Lisbeth's Ghost

"Lizbeth is a tortured girl, bullied from birth, full of hate, full of vengeance, a vengeance not to be held in check for she is capable of intense malice and destruction that must find release as solace for the potentially murderous child.

My kind of girl. Dear to my heart, if I had one.

Her father, Andrew, is an important man with a career not unlike my own, an undertaker, benefiting from others' woes, a man of means who shares none of it with his lonely spinster daughter.

This can all change if Lizbeth succumbs to her late mother, a specter who haunts the poor girl, nudging her toward evil. These specters are a problem for me since I deal with the undead. Specters refuse to accept their fate. Eventually they are corralled back into my employers' fold, though not without resistance.

The positive side of this tale is that our specter encourages the demise of the living. Something I can relate to."

~ G.R.

The face appeared as it always had, protruding from the ceiling in the center of a tile framed by cornice molding as if it were a portrait crafted by a master. A citrus scent filled the room.

Lizbeth stared at the ghoul from her four-poster, unafraid. Why, she had not feared her mother's specter for years, not since 1865 when as a five-year-old, she had run screaming to her father that a ghost appeared before her, spoke to her, introduced herself as her deceased mother, and asked her to perform horrible, unspeakable crimes against him and his new wife. Lizbeth's father dismissed his child as a troublesome, annoying thing and warned her never to speak of the false apparitions in his or his wife's presence again. And she never did.

The ghoul's appendages slashed at the air of the dark bedroom, as if struggling to swim, arms and legs flailing helplessly, reaching for invisible holds to tug its gray torso from out of its plaster prison.

"Lizbeth, pull me through, love. Help your mother to come visit. Take me from the dead and among the living, my sweet, precious child."

But Lizbeth had learned years ago, twenty-five years ago to be precise, that her mother only wanted her to let her guard down in order to—to what? What was the best word to describe what had happened? Combine? Integrate? Become one with Lizbeth? She had once tried to explain the process to her sister, Emma, but like Lizbeth's father and stepmother, Emma dismissed her fears as imaginings, a bit of spoilt food or the hallucinations brought on by the patented elixirs. A child's dreams, but Lizbeth was no longer a child, now a spinster of thirty-two and, by God, not of her own making. Any chance of marriage had been ruined by her tight-fisted father and his ungodly fat wife, Abby Durfee Gray, who insisted Lizbeth call her, "Mother," though Lizbeth would never give her that pleasure.

The insidious ghost moaned as it finally pulled itself free of the obdurate ceiling and now floated gracefully about the darkened room as if blown by zephyrs, the apparition gray, then brown, then coal black. Lizbeth kept guard, knowing her mother could enter her body only from the front. The ghost cried, louder than before, frustrated, each time Lizbeth rolled to block her.

"She plans, my darling daughter. The jezebel plots with your father to rid you from Front Street, from your home. I know this."

Lizbeth sat up, still wary of the slow moving ghost. Her mother had taken over Lizbeth's body only a few times over the years but each instance had ended horribly, the ghost forcing Lizbeth to confront her father and step-mother with ridiculous demands that alienated her family from her. Lizbeth's dead mother's desire for vengeance was so strong there was no telling what she would do if she entered Lizbeth's body again, controlling her daughter's actions and thoughts like a puppet master, Lizbeth helpless to the strings.

"She plans, you say?" Lizbeth asked. "She plots with my loving father to rid me from her, from my house? Please Mother, tell me something I am not aware of if you must keep me from my sleep. My father's obese mongrel has desired my riddance since the day they married."

The ghost dove toward the bed quicker than before. Lizbeth merely turned again on her side.

"Yes, darling, two years past my death, still warm in my grave, he marries Miss Gray as if I never existed. And oh, how I missed my little Lizbeth, so young, two years old. Tell me you remember your mother. Tell me you loved me and missed me. Tell me."

"I was too young."

"Tell me you remember my songs as you suckled, twirling my hair with your pink fingers until it was perfectly curly. Tell me."

"I do not remember. I have had a pleasant day, Mother. Leave me. Go back to the attic and ignore your hateful longings. Abby will die soon enough from age and sickness. She and my father will die soon enough."

But Lizbeth didn't believe they would. She and her sister, both spinsters, had no means of support or any money of their own. Her penny-pincher father spent all on Abby, not them. Lizbeth had depended on David asking for her hand and rescuing her from ending up an old maid, but something had suddenly changed his mind. Was it the paltry dowry? He did not need money and she was still attractive. What made him change his mind?

Her mother hovered on the side of the bed as if sitting on it. She grasped Lizbeth's hair to move it aside the ear, but her hand passed through one side of the head and out the other.

"I can tell you why," the ghost said.

"You read my mind, Mother."

"Yes. Always. And what a sweet thing it is. Your father, my beloved Andrew, lied to your young man."

"He did not."

"Oh, yes. I can see more than just this room, darling. He told your beau that you were not a maiden as the boy expected."

"Why would he do such a thing?"

"The jezebel. She detests you, of course. Since your confrontation, she has hated you to the point that she now plots to rid you from her presence forever. This, I know."

"But it was you, Mother, you inside me, you who fought with her, you who fought with father! I had nothing to do with that!"

"Yes, but that does not matter now. Regardless of fault, she plots your murder. She and Andrew speak of it daily. That is why I am here to warn you, my darling, to help you stop them."

"How?"

"Let me in."

"Never again."

"But I can stop them, love. I can do what your pleasant disposition is incapable of doing. Please let me be in peace knowing I have rid God's world of the evil that would hurt my precious daughter. Let me in."

"No."

"Then ask him. Ask him tomorrow about your beau, and why he would not pay for your coming out and why he makes you and your sister throw slop buckets in the backyard when he has the money to install indoor plumbing. Ask him."

"I will. Now leave."

"And ask him of your pigeons."

"What?"

"Your pigeons."

Lizbeth kept a dozen pigeons cooped up in the barn. They were her pets, her friends, each one named after a Dickens' character, her favorite, Pip, a grey black that pecked affectionately at the birdseed lovingly fed by Lizbeth.

"What of my pigeons?"

"Ask your father. He hates you. They hate you and plot to kill you but you must let me in and we shall kill them first. Let me in. Let me in. Let me in! Let me in!"

"No! Never!" Lizbeth yelled and slapped at the diving ghost, then turned on her stomach each time her mother swooped.

"Let me in!" the apparition screamed again as it slid stealthily under the bed. Lizbeth realized the ploy and quickly rolled onto her back, foiling her mother's clever move.

"Now, go!" Lizbeth yelled.

The ghost seeped out from under the bed, rising slowly to the ceiling, perhaps resigned to its loss.

"Ask him," it said again and disappeared through the ceiling.

The bedroom door opened, her father looming in candlelight.

"What is that confounded din? Do you know the time, Miss? Do you? Your mother and I cannot sleep with your blasted clatter. Please Miss, we beg of you, silence."

Lizbeth sat up in bed. "She is not my mother. My mother died thirty years ago."

"I ask you for your silence, not your insolence. Now nothing more, Miss. Nothing more."

"Did you tell David I was not a maiden?"

"What's that?"

"You heard me perfectly, sir. Did you tell David I was not a maiden?"

"He was not the right man for you. His money was his father's. Not a day's work form him would you get as a husband. We made a correct decision."

"We? Your wife was at this?"

"Your mother . . ."

"She is not my mother!"

Lizbeth's father blew out the candle and as he shut the door said, "We'll speak of this later, at a godly time. Now please, silence."

Lizbeth waited until she heard her father's bedroom door shut, then cried into her hands. How could they do this to her? Her mother had been correct. They had conspired to destroy her, to keep her locked in prison, a spinster, never to laugh, to love, to live. She would have none of it. Tomorrow she would break convention and visit David to tell him the truth. That would end her father's and that wretched stepmother's tyranny.

She lay back to close her eyes, to think of the morrow when suddenly she remembered her pigeons.

It was difficult to leave the house quietly enough without waking Abby and her father. They slept in an adjacent bedroom in their small, poorly made house in Fall River. It may have been possibly the worst built structure in all of Massachusetts, Lizbeth thought. Perhaps the world, but her miserly father could not care a fig what others thought. He amassed a fortune with his funeral parlor yet spent not a dime.

Lizbeth crept quietly from the house and then climbed carefully up the ladder to the barn loft. Would the pigeons cry out and wake her father? "Quiet, my friends. Not a sound from you. It is but I," she whispered.

Lizbeth held the lantern to the coops. They were empty. Outside the cages were her twelve, their heads neatly chopped free of their bodies, the blood still fresh and soaking into the trampled straw. She screamed into her hand and nearly fell from the ladder. No. How could he do such a thing? Kill the only things she had ever loved? She took the bloody hatchet that lay next to the coops and slowly worked her way down the ladder. She would confront him with the weapon tomorrow at breakfast. Perhaps it was Abby who slaughtered her friends, her Pip. Tomorrow, she would know.

* * *

The breakfast was horrid, five-day-old mutton, quenched with spoiled mutton soup. Her father's skinflint ways may kill her with food poisoning before her stepmother does the deed unnaturally. Lizbeth threw the bloody hatchet on the table, spilling the soup.

"What in God's name . . ." Abby said, a large piece of meat muffling her protests.

"That," Lizbeth said, "was the weapon used to destroy my pigeons!" She threw a decapitated pigeon next to the hatchet. Abby screamed. Andrew stood and brushed the bird to the floor.

"What is the meaning of this?"

"You murdered my pigeons," Lizbeth said.

"I did nothing of the kind, Miss."

"You butchered them with that hatchet and left their heads next to my poor dead birds so I would find it. You killed them to spite me."

"I did not. It is true I do not approve of them, since they bring curious neighbor boys who seek mischief, but I did not kill your blasted birds."

Lizbeth grabbed the hatchet. "You did and you told David I was not a maiden and you killed my mother and married a harlot!"

"Well," Abby retorted. "How dare you let her insult me, Andrew."

"I am leaving tomorrow," Lizbeth continued. "I will stay with Emma and her friends and then I will tell David you and your harlot are liars! Good day."

Lizbeth ran up the stairs and slammed the door to her bedroom behind her. She lay on her stomach and had hardly wiped the tears on her pillow when she smelled citrus again. Tangerines perhaps, but it could only mean her mother was near and haunting. Lizbeth did not dare turn over knowing the specter hovered just above her, waiting stealthily to enter her, to become one with her. Lizbeth stayed still, her face buried in the pillow. A mistake, for instantly she felt her mother's icy presence inside her. She shivered and cursed knowing her mother had taken advantage of her distraught state and slipped into her from beneath the bed.

"No, Mother." But Sarah had already taken over the body, Lizbeth now standing, helplessly controlled by the ghost. She walked to the mirror and felt her face.

"It has been so long, my love," the ghost said. "So long since we have been together. However, we have much to do. It is time for the sinners to serve penance. It is time for Andrew and Abby to pay for the untenable cruelty they bestowed upon you and your sister, Emma. It is time, is it not?"

"I will not," Lizbeth said.

"You cannot refuse, my darling. You must do my bidding now but if done willingly it will be much easier. Did he not send David away?"

"Yes."

"Did he not kill Pip?"

"He says not."

"Does he not keep his wealth from you and Emma?"

"Yes, but I will wait, Mother. I must see David. He will understand and take me back once he knows of my father's lies. He will."

Lizbeth reached for the bloody hatchet and admired it, fingering the sharp edge.

"You want them dead," her mother said.

"Yes. However, I do not wish to kill them. I wish to wait, please." Her mother smiled at the mirror forcing Lizbeth's mouth to ape her.

"You have the most beautiful eyes, darling. The harlot, you called her. You must have meant it."

"Yes. I meant it."

Lizbeth put the hatchet on the dresser and began removing her morning clothes. She struggled to stop her hands but the ghost's will was too strong. Soon, she was naked.

"Why?" she asked.

"Blood can be washed from skin, dear, however, it is difficult to remove from clothes. Now let us sit until your father finishes his daily chores at the parlor and the bank. We shall greet him later, when he returns."

Lizbeth sat on the edge of the bed, flipping the hatchet over and over, waiting for Father.

* * *

At 10:45, punctual Father came home and immediately retired to the sitting room downstairs. Lizbeth quickly left her bedroom and before descending the staircase, spied her stepmother sewing on the machine in the guestroom next to Lizbeth's.

"Let us greet Father, darling," her mother's ghost said. "Let us show him our deep affection for his compassion and philanthropy that he has bestowed on his late wife and his children."

Lizbeth opened the sitting room door. Her father lay on the sofa, his hand on his forehead as if in the throes of a headache. He opened his eyes.

"Lizbeth?" He stared incredulously at her. "Good God child, put some clothes on."

Lizbeth moved quickly, raising the hatchet above her head. The blunt side of the weapon came crashing down on his temple, knocking him violently against the armrest. He was conscious—barely, but conscious all the same.

She raised again for another blow. Lizbeth struggled to prevent the attack but her mother's will overcame her.

"It is I, Andrew. Sarah."

"What?" he asked, mumbling, covering his face in anticipation of the next strike.

"Sarah. Your wife, dear. Your victim, but I will not let you take Lizbeth or Emma. No, dear. You must make peace with your God as should your jezebel once I have finished you."

"Lizbeth?" were his last words. The hatchet stuck in the skull, severing the socket with such force it dislodged the eyeball. Ten more times Lizbeth brought the hatchet to its mark until the bloodied face was unrecognizable as that of the miserly Andrew.

Lizbeth's mother wiped the hatchet head across her daughter's stomach, then licked a bit of blood from an index finger as she strode assuredly up the rickety staircase.

"Andrew?" was all Abby managed as the sharp steel split her skull.

"Jezebel! Jezebel! Jezebel!" Lizbeth's screamed with each blow. Nineteen, twenty times the blade struck, Lizbeth trying desperately to close her eyes to the carnage without success as the ghost instead wanted to spy her own handiwork.

Lizbeth turned, exhausted from murder and walked slowly to the doorway where maid Bridgett Sullivan waited, open-mouthed.

"My mother," Lizbeth spit out.

Bridgett looked at Lizbeth, then Abby's corpse and then took the hatchet from Lizbeth.

"Go and wash yourself up, girl," Bridgett said. "I'll clean the floor and take care of the hatchet. Now go!"

Lizbeth walked quickly to the chamber room to wash.

* * *

The detective sat in a chair across from Lizbeth. She stared at him, dispassionately.

"Now, Miss. Your name please."

"Lizbeth," she replied.

He wrote quickly in his notebook.

"Full name, Miss, if you please.

"Lizzie Andrew Borden."

"You said Lizbeth, before."

"That is what I'm called."

"Lizzie your Christian name or is it Elizabeth?"

"I was born, Lizzie."

"Thank you, Miss."

J.J. WHITE

Broccoli Surprise

Published 2011, Helium.com

"Marie and Harold are a bit old to be newlyweds; both previously married to who they thought was their one true love. Alas, as I intimately recall, their mates beat them to the grave-yard and now both Marie and Harold find solace only in each other.

One of them is lying about their past, a past of several spouses or, shall I say, deceased spouses. I'm starting to like where this is going.

I think you will have to read to find out which one of our senior citizens is up to no good. If it were my story, both would be savoring their last meal. Uh oh, spoiler alert. You just can't trust me."

~ G.R.

Marie poured the cream of mushroom soup over the thawed broccoli, then glanced over her shoulder at Harold who was having some difficulty chopping the onions. My, but he just may have been the most handsome man she had ever known and though he was in his sixties, he could easily be mistaken for a younger man. She particularly liked the tinge of salt and pepper hair in his sideburns. Harold's bicep flexed as he pushed down hard on the paring knife.

"Here, try this, Honey," Marie said and handed him a large carving knife.

It sliced through the stubborn Vidalia easier, though his bicep still bulged. Was he purposely flexing it to impress her? Perhaps. But after their last hour of passionate lovemaking he hardly needed to impress her with his physique. She had marveled at his magnificent body as he tenderly caressed her and made her feel young and alive again. After Paul died, she thought she'd never be able to fall in love again, but she had been mistaken. Harold was everything Paul had been and more. Admittedly, she was first attracted to Harold's impressive Lexus sedan and then his fabulous good looks, but eventually it was his kind heart and tender touch that won her over.

She stirred the broccoli and soup together in the casserole dish and added the shredded cheese.

"Are the onions ready, dear?" she asked Harold, who wiped his eyes with a dishtowel.

"I don't know if they're chopped up enough, baby, but my eyes can't take anymore." Harold slid the bowl of chopped onions on the counter next to the casserole dish and wrapped his arms around Marie's waist.

"Haven't you had enough?" she said in mock anger. "My God, you'd think we were honeymooners."

Harold chewed playfully on her earlobe. "No, but technically we are newlyweds, at least for the next six months."

Marie slapped his hands off her with the wooden spoon.

"Go sit down so I can finish this. We'll never eat at this rate."

"What is it again?" Harold asked.

"Broccoli Surprise. An old recipe handed down for generations in my family.

"Generations, huh? I didn't know they had frozen broccoli generations ago."

Marie turned, pecked his lips, and threatened him with the spoon. "I said sit."

Harold sat on a stool at the kitchen island. "What's the surprise in the Broccoli Surprise? Not what I think it is, is it?"

"Stay there and don't get up until I place this in the oven. Understand?"

"Aye, aye, captain," Harold said and played with his Blackberry.

Marie concentrated on the casserole, sprinkling almond slivers over the top. Her eyes began to well up with tears. This had been Paul's favorite dish. She felt terribly guilty, as if she were cheating on him, although he'd been dead for two years. She had promised him on his deathbed that she wouldn't marry again; that she would never love another like she had him. But that was a lie, though she had meant to keep her promise.

She hadn't counted on Harold coming into her life. That night at the country club when she saw him drive up in his car she knew immediately that one day she'd be his wife. Harold was the kindest, gentlest man she'd ever met and like her, had also lost a spouse to a prolonged sickness. God had undoubtedly willed them to be together but Paul was still never far from her mind.

"What is it?" Harold asked.

"What?" Marie sniffed.

"You're crying. The onions aren't that strong. What's bothering you?"

"I was thinking of Paul," Marie said wiping her eyes with the apron. "But it's awful of me to bring him up when you've been so wonderful tonight. I'm sorry, Harold."

"That's okay, I understand. Lots of things still remind me of Sharon. It's only been two years, sweetheart. I can't expect you to just forget someone you were married to for twenty years."

Actually, she had only been married to Paul for a year before he got sick, but she told Harold it was twenty, embarrassed to admit it was her fourth marriage.

"Thank you, dear," Marie said. "It's just that Paul loved . . ."

Harold caressed her shoulders.

She put her hand on his. "Please, sit down," she said. "I'm fine. Just let me finish the casserole."

Harold sat and then said, "Would you mind if I asked what happened to Paul? I mean what he . . ."

"Died of? No, I don't mind. The doctors tried for months to figure it out but the death certificate just said heart failure."

Marie didn't want to tell Harold everything associated with Paul's sickness, the headaches, stomach pain, convulsions, cramps and diarrhea. It was too painful to discuss, all those days and nights she spent tending to his bevy of maladies. Paul was so sick it would be impossible to explain the misery he went through.

"I had him cremated. I didn't want to put him on display in some funeral home. But enough of me. You've said nothing of Sharon."

Harold nodded. "She was my one and only. We met in college, fell madly in love, and never left each other's side until the breast cancer. It's been one year, seven months and three days since she died."

Harold's tears streaked down his cheeks. Marie dabbed them with the dishtowel and hugged him. She kissed the top of his head and went back to the dish, now nearly finished. She pointed to the pantry in the hall. "Be a dear and get me the paprika. It's on the second shelf from the top."

As Harold walked to the pantry, Marie chipped the top of the casserole dish with a large knife to mark her side. She leaned back to check on Harold, then unscrewed the cap off an amber colored bottle the size of a salt shaker.

"Did you find it?" she called out to him.

"Not yet. Still looking. You said the second shelf, right?"

"Yes, dear. Second shelf."

Marie sprinkled white powder on top of one half of the casserole, then covered it with more almond slivers. She slid the dish in the oven. "Never mind, Honey. I think you'll love it like it is."

J.J. WHITE

Grackle Trap

Finalist-2010 California Coast Awards
Honorable Mention, Seven Hills Review *2011*
Short Story Competition
Published in Seven Hills Review *2012, Volume 17*

"Do birds have souls? I can only hope not for if they did my job would be more than I could handle.

A young boy must make a decision that will determine who lives and who dies. I envy that child, myself never having that responsibility; it always left to my supervisors.

Many must make similar decisions sometime in their mortal life, whether to risk losing the love and respect of others by preventing something you know is morally wrong.

I do not have that problem."

~ *G.R.*

Eisenhower was president. Old wars had ended and new ones begun, each crisis more important than the last. But that was their world. My crisis was first grade. My world was school, friends, the backyard, Little League, Mickey Mantle.

Our yard had two acres of uneven, rock-strewn Vermont soil, one acre dormant, filled with delicate birches and strong maples, the other cleared and mown, though full of adventures.

Hours were spent exploring lines of hurried ants traversing

knotholes in the lone poplar, its bark scarred by love oaths of older sisters and brothers knifing their devotion to their latest flame, the initials B.W. loves C.R. through a lopsided heart, pierced by a lopsided arrow. I was jealous, wishing it were my initials of my girlfriend who I would undoubtedly meet when I reached manhood in second grade.

Then, my younger brothers could be jealous.

It was the day my older brother Ben showed me how to catch grackles. The blackbirds filled the cool sky, whirling dervishes of blue, black and gold hues. They grabbed for branches in the tree-walled backyard eyeing the rows of dry corn my sister protected as if she'd given birth to them. Hundreds of blue-necked grackles, white eyed, with cruel black dots for pupils, startled by the slam of the screen door.

Ben jumped the three concrete steps effortlessly, his gloved hand holding a hotdog. Twice my size, almost three times my age, he swaggered down the slope of the septic tank hump toward our burn barrel, a hundred feet from the house.

When he flashed the hotdog to me, I joined the trek, two of my strides for every one of his. I wanted him to hold my hand like he used to on the way to novena but he said I was too old to hold hands anymore and that I shouldn't tell him I loved him, either. I promised I wouldn't.

I glanced over to the O'Brien's yard. Maggie O'Brien ran back and forth in an arc near her house. She was four years old and she wasn't smart. My mother said she was a mongoloid idiot. I didn't know what that was.

Maggie's real name was Margaret, the youngest of seven. My mother said it served the O'Brien's right for having children after the age of forty. I pointed out my mother's pregnancy and how she was thirty-nine and was rewarded with a slap for not knowing the significance of their age difference.

Mrs. O'Brien had tied Maggie to a stump near the back door, one end of a stretchy cord to Maggie's belt, the other end to a metal eyelet that Mr. O'Brien had screwed into the stump. The cord kept Maggie within twenty feet of the house where she could only run in a half circle around the stump, the grass eroded from dirty Keds.

Mrs. O'Brien didn't want Maggie to play with her other children. She kept her outside, except for breakfast, lunch and dinner and sometimes when it rained or snowed. At night, one of Maggie's sisters brought her inside. The next morning she'd be out again, tethered tightly to the stump.

I'd play with her occasionally, but she wasn't very good at it. She drooled too much and when you tried to explain Lincoln Logs, she'd grab you by the head and try to kiss you. One time she chewed on my Yogi Berra rookie card and I didn't play with her for a week.

Ben lifted me over the burn barrel so I could see inside, ash floating out into the thin breeze. We burned everything in the barrel, trash, garbage, wood, grass. If you stood too close, the flames seared your eyebrows and eyelashes off. Mine always grew back darker and longer.

He held the hotdog above his head, getting the full attention of the menacing birds, their songs interrupted. "You let them see it first," he said, his muscles flexing in his T-shirt as he rotated, the gladiator teasing the hoard in the tree coliseum. "Some can smell it J-Dub, I'm pretty sure of it, but grackles are smart. We don't want to catch the smart ones though, do we?"

I nodded in awe. "We want to catch the stupid ones, like those." I pointed to three birds in a birch, their talons tight around a branch.

Ben shrugged and said, "Watch." He threw the hotdog in the barrel and slid the metal cover half on, leaving a semi-circle opening. We stepped back to the poplar to wait. Some of the grackles left their perch in a feint, stopping short of the curious barrel, then shooting back to their perch, safe once again from sure death.

But Ben was right. Two grackles couldn't overcome their hunger and dove rocket-like into the barrel. He sprinted to the trap, with me close behind, and pushed the lid over the top. One bird escaped through a hole in the side but the other was too fat, its wings flapping in desperation against the sides. Ben lifted me over his head and threw me in the air in triumph, then caught me, as we spun together until I was dizzy.

Before I could stand up straight, he handed me about four feet of thin cord, pushed the lid back, and reached in with his gloved hands. The grackle pecked and clawed fiercely at the gloves, its muscular body wriggling in Ben's grip.

"Tie the cord to its claw," he said, and held one of the bird's feet out to me. I was afraid of it. What if it clawed my hand? He reassured me by isolating the bird foot with two fingers. With talons held immobile, I tied the cord and pulled tight a knot skillfully learned in Cub Scout Pack 17, earlier that year.

Ben gestured with his head to the rusty hole near the top of the barrel. "Tie it through there," he said. "And hurry up, my hands are getting tired."

I used the same knot for the hole. When Ben released the grackle, it flew directly for the trees, but four feet or so from the barrel it came to an abrupt stop, nearly ripping its talon off. It wouldn't do that again. I knew that and I was only six.

We backed off as the bird perched on the rim of the barrel for a few seconds, then flew off, but with less effort, as if it knew the pain to be had from an escape. It was a pitiful thing to watch, the graceful black bird hovering above the barrel, the cord stretched to its limit.

I turned to glance at Maggie, she also tugging on her cord at the end of its reach. She jumped, then yelled, then began her semi-circle run, back and forth, her ever-present smile glistening in the sunlight. Monotonous—to everyone but her.

Ben punched me playfully. "Tomorrow we'll take turn with the pellet gun. You want to try it with me, big fella? It's about time Dad took you hunting with us."

I tried to agree with a worried smile but was distracted by the grackle's caws and Maggie's screeches. I nodded and turned toward the house. I wanted to eat some macaroni and cheese and turn up the volume on the TV.

I had seen Ben and his friends kill trapped grackles before. They would line up near the back of the house, taking turns with the pellet gun. At first, the grackle would fly to the end of the cord to escape but after a few hits of shot, it would take shelter in the barrel. It was my job to kick the barrel and spook the grackle out for another round of gunfire. Eventually there'd be a successful headshot and the bird would topple off the barrel and hang upside down a few inches from the ground, its blue plume matted with blood. Tomorrow it would be my turn. As I shut the screen door, Maggie jumped from the stump, oblivious.

The quiet of the night broke with the squawk of the bird, the flap of wings against the air, against the barrel. Maggie screamed as each pellet hit, blood dripping over her smile as she hung upside down. I didn't sleep well.

The next morning I stood in the backyard against the wall of the house, my attention riveted on the desperate grackle, flapping its wings slowly in its shallow hover, exhausted by its night attempts at escape. Then I turned to watch Maggie gleefully running in her half-moon race to nowhere. Smiling. Smiling.

My head swiveled between the grackle and Maggie, then back to the grackle, and then to Maggie. I walked over and untied the cord.

J.J. WHITE

𝕮𝖍𝖊 𝕮𝖍𝖎𝖓𝖊𝖘𝖊 𝖀𝖓𝖉𝖊𝖗𝖙𝖆𝖐𝖊𝖗

Published 2011, Helium.com

"Something odd is out there in the Chinese waters, something man-made, yet life-like, perhaps more pet than human. It has murdered one hundred and fifty, sent them to their watery grave where I shall salvage their souls for, how shall I put it, redistribution in eternity.

Our stoic hero, Detective John Tang, suspects the diminutive and submissive undertaker, Cheng Lee, is behind these mysterious deaths. How could that be? Mr. Lee seems the most unlikely of all Zao-Zhis millions who could have committed these marvelous crimes.

I suggest you read this shallow and rather poorly written tale if for no other reason than to tally the dead as I did. It at least breaks up the tedium of my waiting for the likes of you."

~ G.R.

Zao Zhi Harbor, China—Year 2042

The large ferryboat skimmed across the water on its pontoons at two hundred and twenty knots, nearly completing its sixty-kilometer trip in less than fifteen minutes. It slowed to twenty knots for the one kilometer left to the harbor. The pontoons sank off the surface into the oil-soaked bay and the one hundred and fifty or so riders in the enclosed upper area passenger lounge walked out on the deck to enjoy the light breeze off the water.

Five hundred meters to the portside of the ferry, a peculiar looking circular cloud seemed to hover just above the water. To disinterested onlookers, it looked like an innocent cloud of diesel smoke but had they inspected more closely they would have seen millions of tiny black mosquito sized objects swirling one behind the other, creating the effect of a ten meter wide whirlwind.

Suddenly, as if responding to an order, the cloud of black atoms aligned themselves in perfect order into the shape of a huge javelin. With a tremendous blast of air and water, the spear bolted skyward, high into the air, until it reached the apogee of its flight and then reversed course straight down into the bay. Traveling at nearly the speed of sound, it turned just below the surface and raced toward the underside of the ferryboat.

No one on board saw or heard the projectile but when the boat listed forty degrees to the port, immediate panic ensued as the huge hole in its hull sucked in seawater.

The ferryboat sank in seconds, dragging down motorcycles, automobiles, and all but a few passengers into the putrid dark bay.

About a kilometer away, on the starboard side of where the boat had once been, a large black arrow surfaced from the bay, reformed into a swirling dark cloud, and sped off toward the green hills behind the port.

Three days later, the old undertaker, Cheng Lee, sat quietly at a small table erected on the rear lawn of his funeral home. He sipped his tea and contemplated the work still left on the three corpses laid out on tarps nearby.

He had processed twenty-two bodies that day, and though very tired, he thought he must finish the last three out of respect for the families. As he was about to return to his work, he saw a police car drive up the mountain road toward him. The car hovered several feet above the road, the wash from its underside jets propelling dirt on either side. As it came to a stop next to him, he was able to make out its occupant. It was John Tang, the middle-aged detective of the provincial police department, whom he knew from webzine accounts of the detective's exploits with city criminals. Cheng Lee was honored by the unexpected visit.

Detective Tang pushed a button on the console and the large Plexiglas sphere split in two, allowing him to climb out of the hover car to greet the old man.

"Please," the undertaker said. "Have tea with me, Detective."

"So, you know who I am. Then you must know why I am here."

"I do know you from your fame, sir, but I do not know the reason for your visit. Tea?"

"Yes, please," the detective replied, and he sipped the hot green tea.

"Very refreshing. I assume you are Mr. Lee, the proprietor?"

"Yes," the old man said, bowing his head slightly. "I began the unfortunate business of preparing the departed in 2002 and as you see, I am still at it, forty years later."

"Yes, yes, a miserable job, like mine. Old man, you know of the ferryboat sinking three days ago in the harbor, No?"

"Of course I do," he said, pointing to the corpses. "These three are the last of the poor souls. I was about to process them when you arrived. Why do you ask?"

The detective wiped his mustache and continued. "We have had two disasters in as many months in ZaoZhi and I believe that to be too much of a coincidence for such a small harbor town. Last month a hillside gave way, as you know, killing forty-two valley dwellers, and now, this ferryboat sinking with more than a hundred and fifty deaths. I have to ask myself, as a detective, are these coincidences or could it be a premeditated and diabolical scheme. I would also ask myself who would benefit most from these disasters. How many bodies have you processed from these incidents?"

"Eighty-three," the undertaker said.

"Yes—eighty-three and what are you paid for each?"

Mr. Lee rubbed his bald head in thought. "I receive 30,000 for copper, 40,000 for silver, and 50,000 for gold."

"Explain yourself, old man. What do you mean by this copper and gold business?"

"Oh, yes," the old man laughed. "Of course you don't understand. It is the nano-technology that confuses you. Come here, let me show you."

He walked the detective over to the three bodies and pointed at a dark swirling cloud next to them.

"As you know," he continued, "in the past few decades, because of the scarceness of cemetery property, the bodies were either cremated or processed and then formed into epoxy bricks for display by the families. Since cremation has been outlawed, we undertakers are only allowed to process the corpses. This was not a tidy business, as you well know. The crushing and grinding of human skeletons and tissue was a tedious and time-consuming chore and was met with much dissatisfaction by the remaining family members. Now, I have purchased a splendid nano-processor made up of millions of tiny organisms that can be programmed into the shape of a giant machine that will process a body, remove and expel all the fluids, and deliver a solid brick of remains, no bigger than a loaf of bread, all in a matter of seconds."

"Yes, yes," the detective said impatiently, "but what of the gold and silver you talked about?"

"Well, sir. Why not let me just show you, if you'll assist me. My help has left for lunch and has not returned."

The old man pulled a dirty sheet off a pile of two-meter, thin copper rods. He removed one rod from the pile and strapped it to a bamboo pole that had been driven into the ground. With the rod secured, he uncovered a bloated corpse and grabbed its naked shoulder and leg. He motioned for the detective to do likewise, which Detective Tang did, looking as if he might retch from the smell. Together they lifted the body up against the pole.

The old man strapped the body to the bamboo and copper rod poles with reeds until it was suspended in the upright position. He looked at the detective and said, "Watch, now."

He barked a few commands at the hovering nano-cloud and stepped back, pulling the detective with him. The cloud burst into the sky, high above the two men and formed a wide funnel that was at least ten meters high. Detective Tang watched awestruck as the cloud created thousands of small rotating blades inside the cone.

The undertaker barked another command and the giant machine, now resembling an enormous sea cucumber, dropped down over the corpse and the two rods. There was a high-pitched whine as the blades obliterated the three objects, followed by a low hum and finally a piercing bang. Suddenly, there was the loud sound of escaping gas, and a small blood-colored cloud puffed out of the top of the unearthly machine and floated toward a large pink-tainted outcrop of trees.

Near the bottom of the great cone, the atoms reformed into a box. Detective Tang watched wide-eyed as a door opened underneath the box and out dropped a copper-colored brick. He walked over, picked it up, and read the inscription: Chen Long Do, 2005-2042, at rest forever.

The old man took the brick from the detective and placed it on top of a pile of other bricks nearby that were covered by a green tarp.

"That was copper. I do the same in gold or silver if the family can afford it."

"I see," Detective Tang said. "Very lucrative for you, no doubt, old man. I think you will be very rich if these calamities continue to befall our fellow citizens. I am leaving now, sir. I won't hold you and your malevolent machine from completing your morbid task but you will see me soon. My investigation will show what I have concluded already, that you are somehow involved in these outrageous disasters. I will see you, very soon."

The detective walked hurriedly to the hovercraft and stared straight ahead as the plastic dome shut over the top of him. The large sphere lifted off the ground, turned on its axis and, within seconds, sped down the road and out of sight.

Cheng Lee looked down at the black cloud, now winding between his legs, and spoke softly. "I believe Detective Tang means to do us harm, lotus petal. Go stop him now, my dear, before he does something foolish."

The cloud shot off in the direction of Detective Tang like a bloodhound fresh on the scent of a fox. A kilometer down the road it reformed into a huge wall and dropped directly in front of the shocked detective. The plastic bubble car cracked in half as it smashed into the impenetrable wall, propelling Detective Tang into the soft air bags. He screamed as he looked up to see the wall metamorphose into a huge cone, twice the size of the one he witnessed ripping the corpse of Chen Long Do. The cone dropped over the car, muffling the sounds of the sharp blades tearing at the car and its hapless occupant.

The cloud reformed into the shape of a saucer and flew jet-like toward the funeral home. It stopped just a meter from the undertaker and dropped a translucent brick out of its side onto the ground. The undertaker picked up the still warm brick and observed the inscription. Curiosity killed the cat.

He waved his hand lovingly through the cloud of black atoms and said, "Very fitting, my lotus petal."

Much Quieter in the House

Published 2011, Helium.com

"Regardless of how hard you try to raise your children properly they don't always turn out as you had hoped. I should know. I raised four of the little ones by myself and despite my best intentions, one of them turned out good. An abomination, seized by the enemy and raised above, white wings and all. Sickening.

Liz Young raised Heather to be a good girl and yet there she was in the online newspaper mug shots, a common criminal, a wicked wicked girl. Like my ex-wife. Determined to right her wrong, Liz begs her husband, Sam, to help her adopt another little girl to see if she can get it right this time, raise the child properly. Despite the cost, Sam agrees and then Liz is happy and Sam is happy because Liz is happy. That happiness may be a bit premature.

The death in this tale is implied. Implied by me."

~ G.R.

In the bottom right hand corner of the local newspaper's website was a thumbnail mugshot of Heather.

Liz Young had just hoped to catch up on the national news she had missed while vacationing with her husband, Sam, on Florida's Space Coast. The hotel computer had been available the last four days, but she had wanted no interference from computers or cell phones or even the TV to distract from their much-needed vacation. But then there was Heather, looking older than her twenty-eight years, the eyes sorrowful, as if saying, "Mom, help me."

Liz made sure no one was waiting behind her to use the lobby computer and then clicked on the icon.

There was the daughter she hadn't seen in five years, the daughter who had dropped out of college to live with a man of suspect intentions, the daughter Liz had nursed, taught, held and loved, the daughter who had left the only two people in the world who had loved her.

Liz adjusted her reading glasses to get a closer look at her baby. Heather looked so—what was it? Tired? Yes, tired. She looked tired and hopeless. There was a caption underneath the mugshot but she wouldn't read it, couldn't read it. She knew what it said. Heather Young, 28, arrested 10/12/2011 for possession of a controlled substance or perhaps for solicitation of prostitution, it didn't matter what it said, she couldn't bear to read it. It hurt too much.

Heather looked desperate, streaks of mascara staining her cheeks. She had been crying. But why? Because of the arrest, or was it something more, something deep in her daughter's heart that cried out for help?

Liz wiped her eyes and wished to go back in time to the day of Heather's birth, when she held her to her breast and kissed the pink soft spot on her tiny head.

What had she done wrong? Why had it ended up like this? Her beautiful baby, arrested, perhaps addicted to those awful drugs the young seemed to crave. First Matthew and now Heather. It made Liz question her God. Only for a moment, but the doubt was there.

Sam leaned over her shoulder. She quickly shut down the page.

"Who was that, Honey?" Sam pecked Liz's neck with a little kiss. How wonderful to have such a man for a husband. She tried to be a good wife to him and she thought she was. So why had she failed so miserably as a mother?

"No one," she said. "Just another lost celebrity, you know."

"Um," he said. "Let's go try out the clean sheets." He rubbed her shoulders. Fifty-eight years old and still acting like that boy in the '73 pickup truck at make-out point on that foggy Iowa Lake. Some men just never grew up.

She stood from the computer and hugged the tall, lanky Sam, her truck driver, lean, muscular, still attractive in his Levis and plaid, long-sleeve shirt, and yet despite his intimidating presence, a real pussycat. How she loved her Sam.

She sighed. Why did she have to see that mug shot of Heather today of all days?

"What's wrong?" Sam said. He turned her to face him.

"Nothing."

"Don't tell me that. We've been married thirty-six years and—"

"Thirty-seven."

"Thank you, Liz. Thirty-seven and I know that sigh. Something's wrong."

"It's just—I was thinking about the kids and I—well, you know."

"Matt wasn't your fault." He pulled her close to him, his long arms folding around her as if she were a child with skinned knees. She didn't deserve this man. "If anything," he continued, "it was my fault. I was never there when he needed me. Oh, for Christ's sake I was two thousand miles away when he. . . ."

Liz cried into his shirt, staining the pocket. Bystanders gawked and then quickly turned their heads back, embarrassed. Sam walked her over to a comfortable sofa in the corner of the lobby, then lifted her chin.

"Look at me, Liz. Look at me."

She smiled, closed mouth, but he would know it was for his sake. She couldn't hide her feelings with him, she never could.

"You did everything for the kids. You gave up your job. You fed them, read to them, helped them whenever they needed help. You were there when I was hauling pigs to Texas or wherever."

"I know, Sam, but—I can't understand it. You're right, we did—I did everything I thought was right and it wasn't enough. First Matthew and the overdose and now Heather and her problems and—"

"You've seen her."

Liz dropped her gaze. Why had she even mentioned Heather?

"No. I just thought she might be in trouble, you know, because of the drugs—"

"You did see her. Are you giving her money again?"

"No, Sam. I'm not."

"You are."

"No. I swear. I haven't seen her since the trial."

"I don't believe you."

"Well, I'm sorry. I shouldn't have said anything. I'm sorry, but it's not fair. Other parents were much worse than us and their children are fine. Their kids are happy and married. So why did ours turn out this way? Explain it to me, Sam. Why?"

"I don't know. Maybe nothing would have helped. I read somewhere that regardless of the parents' efforts and environment, kids still go bad. Maybe it's genetics. Maybe a bad gene skipped one of us and landed in Matt and Heather. Who knows? Who the hell knows?"

She stood and kissed Sam's cheek. "Maybe that's it, honey, and that's why I want to try again."

"You're joking, right? Check your license. Your birth year is the same as mine."

"That's not what I mean. I want to adopt. If it's genetics, then what better way to overcome them then with an adoption? I want a baby, Sam. A baby girl to love again. This time it'd be different, I know it would."

Sam shook his head. "Do you know what that would cost? I'm getting ready to retire. That's the stupidest thing you've ever said. We'll barely get by on the pension and social security in a few years and you want to raise another child?"

"You don't have to call me stupid."

"I didn't call you stupid. I said it was a stupid idea and it is. What is she going to feel like in twenty years when we're dead? Have you thought about that?"

Liz stood and wiped her eyes with a tissue from her purse.

"I'm not going to be dead in twenty years and even if I were she'd be old enough to be on her own by that time. You don't know what it's like to see your babies become criminals when you tried so hard to raise them. I want another chance, Sam. I want to do it right this time and I'll do it by myself if I have to."

"Let's not fight about it," he said. "We'll go up to the room and rest before touring the Space Center. We can discuss it later."

The great compromiser. It was one of the things about Sam that pissed her off. Whenever they argued he'd try to calm her down, not because he really wanted to discuss it later but in hopes she'd forget about it. Well not this time.

"No. I want a baby girl. I don't care what it costs."

"We can't afford it. It could cost thousands. Tens of thousands. We need that money. We need it to retire."

"I don't care. I've looked it up. We can get a white baby in two months if we pay the adoption agency the premium."

"And how much is that?"

"Fifty thousand."

"Dollars?"

"No, drachmas, Sam. Yes, dollars. We have it. I've seen the accounts."

Sam flung his arms over his head. The gawkers all looked as one.

"It's impossible. I'd have to tap into the 401 K. I'm not going to do that. What about a black baby or Hispanic? How much do they cost?"

Liz sat down again, if he's asking about price, then she had him.

"Five or six thousand but I want a white baby. It's not fair to the children to raise them in a family of a different race. When they're older, they'd feel like no one accepted them, white or black."

"You're an expert now?"

"I'm not backing down. I want a baby—a white girl and this time she's going to love me and I'm going to love her."

She gently held Sam's hands. "I want her to be a friend to me when she grows up. I didn't have that with Matt. I don't have it with Heather. Please, honey."

Sam said nothing. He walked over to the lobby window and stared out at passing cars. When he came back to the sofa, Liz saw it in his eyes.

"I'll look into it," he said.

* * *

The $50,000 turned out to be $70,000. Sam had to cash in the entire 401 K. It was worth $160,000 but with penalties and Uncle Sam's cut he just made the $70,000. He slid the check across the desk to the lawyer. She read the amount and smiled.

Sam felt uncomfortable in the office, underdressed to say the least. What difference did it make though, he wasn't trying to impress Ms. Candace Taylor-Mann, Esquire, a member of the American Academy of Adoption Attorneys or so the certificate on her wall stated. No, he was there to buy a baby girl for his uncompromising wife, a woman he loved more than life itself. So what if they'd have to live on oatmeal and macaroni the rest of their lives. So what?

"Well," said Ms. Taylor-Mann. "This is all you and Liz have to do. From now on, I'll get the ball rolling."

"How long?" Sam said.

"A few weeks if everything goes all right. If there's any complications, then there may be more fees assessed."

"That's it, Miss. If there's more fees accessed, then someone else will have to come up with the money. Maybe after I've made a few runs south, but not for a while."

The lawyer stood, straightened her skirt and held out her hand.

"Oh, I'm sure everything will be fine. We'll call you and Liz as soon as we have the baby."

"How old is it again?"

"About six months. We'll receive the child from the mother next week."

"Okay, thanks." Sam shook her hand and left.

He'd cherish the look on Liz's face later when he told her that in a few weeks they'd have the baby girl she'd asked for. But why hadn't he held his ground and told her no? He knew why. He loved her too much to refuse her anything.

He had been fortunate to get the girl. The state told him they wouldn't allow adoptions to anyone over forty. It was the same with the church. So his only option was with a licensed private adoption agency. They said they would relax the rules on the age of the adopting parents as long as the clients had the cash. Anything can be bought with enough money. Even love.

* * *

Liz lifted the child in her arms and smothered her with kisses. She didn't know who to kiss more, the baby or Sam.

"She's pretty big for six months," Sam said.

"Oh, she's just fine, just right. Aren't you, darling?" The girl tried to wriggle out of Liz's arms to get to the toys on the floor. When Liz straightened her back up, the girl cried.

"She's got good lungs," Sam said. "I don't feel so bad about leaving you now with that racket."

Liz rocked the baby until she quieted. "It's probably an upset tummy or maybe she's tired. A nap will help."

Sam nodded. "Maybe she misses her mother."

Liz stared hard at him. "I'm her mother."

"I didn't mean any—"

"I know you didn't. But she needs to know I'm her mother now. I'm not going to make the same mistake I made with Matt and Heather. Not with my little—" She looked up at Sam. "We haven't named her yet, have we?"

"The lawyer said it's Cheryl."

"Not anymore," Liz said.

Sam lifted his suitcase and leaned over to kiss Liz, and then the baby, who had begun to fuss again. "You'll come up with something. I've got to go if I want to get to Toledo by nightfall."

"We have to name her first."

"Okay—what do you like?"

"Samantha," she said.

"But that's Sam like mine. A bit confusing don't you think?"

"No. She'll always be Samantha and you'll always be my Sam."

She placed the baby on the carpet then stretched up on her toes to hug him. Samantha cried louder until Liz picked her up. They walked Sam to the foyer.

"Got to go," he said. "See you both Friday."

She lifted Samantha to the window and waved the little girl's hand at her new father. Sam ground the gears of his semi as he drove away down the dirt road, a brown cloud cloaking the big rig.

Samantha continued to cry, sometimes wheezing for breath before renewing the high-pitched wail. What was wrong with her? She'd had almost an entire bottle of formula. Maybe it was the new environment. The child would just have to adapt. Liz took Samantha to her bedroom and placed her in her crib. The child screamed louder, her face now a bright red.

"Now stop, Samantha. Stop it or you'll get sick. Stop it."

It was hopeless. She was just like Matt and Heather, always crying, always wanting attention. She had spoiled her children and for what? All it did was make them want more until there was no more and then Matt kills himself and Heather, well Heather was doing the same thing, wasn't she?

No, Liz would not spoil Samantha. This time the child would be a normal child and a loving child. This time Liz would get it right.

Samantha screamed, flailing at the blanket wrapped between her legs.

"You have to stop it, Samantha," Liz pleaded. "Now please. I mean it, darling."

But it was no use. She left the screaming child and calmly walked through the kitchen to the isolation of the utility room where even there the cries penetrated through the walls. Liz searched Sam's workbench until she found what she needed. Samantha's din had subsided to pitiful sobs, but as soon as Liz stepped in the nursery, Samantha renewed her loud cries.

Liz sat the child up in the crib and placed a strip of duct tape across her mouth. The child's eyes went wide with fear as she screamed muffled cries at her new mother.

"There, now. Maybe you'll learn to stop crying when Mommy tells you to."

Liz went to the kitchen and made herself a sandwich for lunch. She thought it was much quieter in the house now. Yes, much quieter.

Against the Dying of the Light

Honorable Mention Writers Digest *80th Annual Writing Competition*

"The title of this piece has been, how can I say it, lifted—yes—lifted from that morose peach of a poet, Dylan Thomas. It is a line from his "Do Not Go Gentle Into That Good Night." I am not surprised the author would steal from the talented, his morals and skills comparable to that of a common thief. Still, the title is in itself the best part of the tale.

Our unlikely protagonist is an old man suffering the agony and frustration of macular degeneration. Despite his malady, he manages to throw all he owns into winning the heart of an attractive and quite rich doctor. Yes, I find that hard to believe also. The man is determined though, and one must give the old geezer credit for his effort.

His success ends in a death not entirely undeserved. And as the title of this book promised, there is a twist. Perhaps you should read the last paragraph first to save time."

~ G.R.

The lights hurt his eyes, fluorescent bursts that stung like saltwater if he happened to gaze up at them, the intensity not from their brilliance but of his own worsening macular degeneration.

He played leapfrog with his index finger over an eyebolt fastened securely to a steel table. A lot of steel in the small room, steel walls, steel chair, steel door. He poked an ashtray. Burn marks on the green vinyl tabletop bore out its use. Unusual for the times. Ashtrays made him nostalgic for the good days, when everyone smoked, when Isabel and he lived on a motorcycle, when he could see a gnat's ass from a hundred feet away.

It was considerate of them not to shackle him. That meant they were staring at him, though, and he didn't like them staring at him. He gazed up at the two-way mirror. They think they have it figured out, nothing left but the confession to wrap up and then find a local bar to get shitfaced. Well—maybe. But then again, he's had more time to think about it than they have.

* * *

George pressed hard on the stapler, but the photocopy of Dr. Kathryn Peregrine's face fell from the wall to the floor of his bedroom. He stepped down the ladder to retrieve more staples from a kitchen drawer. Isabel had bought the staples six years ago at a discount store thinking the two of them would be dead before they ran out. She was right of course. She had died two years earlier and he was in his mid-sixties. Perhaps he'd be gone soon, but he still had much to do and had yet to see Kathryn.

After refilling the stapler, George went back to his task. Kathryn's pictures covered the back bedroom wall except the area behind his headboard. The bed was too large to move. There were three walls left to do and he estimated about six hundred photocopies still in the cardboard box. About four hundred Kathryns smiled sincerely at him from his wall. She was one of the most beautiful women he had ever met, though the meeting was brief and professional, but even then, he was in awe of her stunning good looks.

The photo had been taken without her knowledge at a physician's convention in Orlando. She had been flirting with a fellow doctor in the hallway during a break when George snapped her mid-laugh.

The girl at the copy center had looked confused, or surprised, or maybe suspicious, when he ordered a thousand laser copies of the photo. Why do you need a thousand copies of the woman's face? her eyes asked. But it was none of her goddamn business.

George retrieved the escaped Kathryn from under the bed and stapled it over the remaining square of exposed drywall.

He needed about fifty thousand dollars to fuel his quest, to achieve his goal, that is, to meet and hopefully get to know Dr. Peregrine. Tomorrow, he would go downtown and negotiate with a representative of one of those rip-off finance companies that buy out your pension payments with a lump sum amount. His payments came to twenty thousand a year, so figuring he'd live another ten years, his pension was worth two hundred thousand to those clowns. They'd offer him thirty thousand and he'd take it. That was the amount he needed to join the private golf club, the club that Kathryn belonged to. It was a lot of money to meet a woman, but she wasn't just any woman. He had to belong to her inner circle. He needed to get to know her socially since their worlds were so different.

After he had the thirty thousand, he'd sell the RV. With his eyesight, he couldn't drive it anymore and he'd need the income to maintain the façade, to give the appearance of a man with money. It was the only way to be with her.

Tuesday morning, George handed the certified check for thirty-three thousand to the manager of the Rio Pinar Country Club. Thirty thousand for the membership and three thousand for the annual dues. Despite the cost, George would still have to pay forty dollars for the rental of a golf cart, each time he played.

Through the large window of the manager's office, George admired the pristine golf club, of which he was now a member. All part of the image, an image of a wealthy retiree, a widower, lonely for companionship. The manager grinned and shook George's hand. There were few new members at the private club because of the poor economy. Perhaps that was why the man hadn't asked for references.

George watched Kathryn through the window. White petals from a row of dogwoods blew onto the practice putting green where she worked on a difficult right to left putt before her round. She was a member of the Pine Pounders, a Tuesday league that boasted at least four, single digit handicap players, including the lovely Dr. Peregrine. She wore a lime green polo shirt tucked tightly into a beige skirt, hemmed two inches above her tanned knees. The blond hair was braided neatly under a white Titleist visor that rested comfortably on large Ray Bans. Two older men watched her surreptitiously as a handsome pro, perhaps ten years younger than she, helped with her grip. More than once, she pressed her hip against him, smiling each time. What would Mr. Peregrine say?

Kathryn slid into the golf cart and drove to the first tee. George had to squint as everything turned to a blur the farther away she got from him. His eyes worsened every day. Kathryn was completely out of focus as she took a few practice swings, but George imagined her breasts lifting as she took a few cleansing breaths and then peppered the golf ball long and straight down the fairway. Was she smiling? It was good if she was. She had so little time left.

* * *

It had been a month since George had joined the club. In that time, he had gotten to know some of the members. Kathryn was elusive, rarely at the club except on Tuesday for her league and some weekends late at the bar where she drank several vodka martinis and usually went home with the most attractive man in the lounge. George knew he would never be that man. He was twenty years her senior and nearly blind, though he would probably surprise her if they ever hooked up, as she liked to call it.

The only way to be alone with her would be on the golf course. He concentrated on that plan. The Pine Pounders refused his application to their league, since George could barely break a hundred, so he joined a Saturday men's league where he could find a partner with better eyesight than him, to help him improve his game. Paul Jacobs stood behind George each time he hit a ball and told him where it landed.

When George thought his game was good enough, he approached Kathryn. "Dr. Peregrine," George said as he sat down beside her at the bar. She continued to sip her martini then turned her head toward George, nearly impaling herself with the toothpick that poked out of the olive. She said nothing, raised her eyebrows, and then turned back to the martini.

"I know you from somewhere, don't I?" she asked her olive.

George proffered his hand. She ignored it. "George Carter." Not his real surname of course. "New member, about a month now. I've met just about everyone in the club."

His gaze dropped to her breasts as she dabbed at some spilled drink in her cleavage and then sucked on her finger. She was forty-five, married twice, no children and had been practicing fifteen years as an orthopedic surgeon.

She licked her glass and glanced back at George. "I've seen you before." She pointed at him. "In the hospital, maybe? You have back problems or is it just the eyes?"

George smiled. Not really an astute observation because of his coke bottle lenses, but not bad for someone after four martinis. They were alone. Alas, no one for her to go home with.

"No," he said. "You may have seen me around the club. I tried to get into your league but they wouldn't let me."

Kathryn poked his chest. It was like an electric shock. She burped loudly. "That's because you suck, just like all the old men around here. Right, Barry?"

The bartender nodded. "They all suck—not like you, Kate."

"That's right. I don't suck. At least not in golf anyway." She stirred the martini with her finger and stared back at George.

"You still here, Gene?"

"George."

"Yeah, okay. What do you want, George? I have to get to bed early tonight. Surgery tomorrow. Another old fart bitching and moaning about his L4. Sick of it, you know?"

"May I buy you another?"

"No." She sipped the last of the drink "Okay, yeah, you may." She held up the glass. "Barry—Gene here wants to buy me another. Thinks he can get lucky or something."

"Not at all, Kathryn," George said. "I was wondering if you'd like to play a round of golf sometime. Maybe a weekend."

Kathryn exchanged glasses with Barry. "You and me? You're not my type. I still have a few eggs left. Check out some of those dried out old hags in the Monday league. Take the pick of the litter. Right, Barry?" Barry smirked and wiped glasses.

"Let me explain," George said. "I'm trying to play at least one round with each member. Get to know everyone that way. Just one round."

"Then you'd leave me alone?"

"Yes."

Kathryn gulped the last of the drink. "Tuesday, after lunch." She held up a finger. "One round."

"Yes—that's fine. Tuesday. I'll remind you after your league. Thank you."

She slid the empty glass to Barry who caught it a foot from the floor. "Call me a cab, barkeep. I am fucking drunk." She plopped down in an upholstered chair near the dining room.

* * *

The next Tuesday, George waited outside the pro shop. He checked the clock that stood on a pedestal near the practice green. Two p.m.

Would she remember? He'd give her ten more minutes then try to flush her from the bar. Hopefully, she hadn't drunk too much.

He was tired. He'd spent hours the previous night painting red heart outlines around Kathryn's face on all of the photocopies stapled to his walls. Then he filled out pages in a diary professing his undying love for the surgeon. Finally, he had spent a half-hour cutting out his face from an old photo and gluing it next to a photo of Kathryn's face and then placing it in a silver frame he'd bought from a gift shop. Engraved below the faux photo were the words, "Kathryn and George."

Kathryn emerged from the clubhouse carrying a clear plastic bag holding ice and four cans of beer. She waved, shook his hand, and placed the beer in a cooler attached to the golf cart.

"Barry mentioned I may have said a few things Saturday night that were cruel," she said. "I hope you forgive me, um—"

"George," he said. "George Carter, and no, you were wonderful and funny. May I get your bag?" George pointed to her cart. He walked over to it quickly.

"We could each take a cart if you want," she said.

"No, no, don't be silly. Let's share. That way we can get to know each other."

On the first tee, Kathryn popped open two beers and handed one to George. By the third hole, she had opened two more.

"I'll get us refills at the ninth," she said.

She was an excellent golfer. Her short game was as good as her long one. When she missed a green, she'd get up and down deftly, rarely bogeying a hole. George played worse than usual. He had other things on his mind. From the first tee, he'd thought only of the seventeenth hole. His heart raced in anticipation of what he was about to do.

The booze had slowed their pace of play, which worked to his advantage. By the time they had reached the seventeenth, the course was nearly empty. The sky glowed shades of orange as the sun began to set. They wouldn't finish the round but not because of darkness.

Kathryn had one hundred and fifty yards to the green. She placed the can of beer on the tee box and smacked a seven iron, ten feet from the flag.

"Not bad for playing in the dark, right, George?" She rubbed his shoulder affectionately and placed the club in her bag. As soon as she sat in the cart, George slammed the pedal to the floor and steered for a large retention pond on the right side of the fairway. Before Kathryn could yell out, they hit the water hard. It was four feet deep in the middle. George knew that from two weeks earlier when he had waded in to gauge the depth. He explained later in the clubhouse that he had accidentally fallen in trying to retrieve a ball. A lie everyone believed, aware of George's bad eyesight.

The cart flipped on its side, dumping them into the pond. Kathryn stood almost immediately and yelled in frustration to the empty course. George hooked his arm around her neck and pulled her under water. She slapped at him as he knelt on her chest, working against her athletic ability and natural buoyancy to keep her under.

George pushed her shoulders against the pond bed stretching to keep his head above water. When Kathryn's movements became less frenetic, he stood on her chest and then counted to a hundred before stepping off.

* * *

Two detectives came into the interview room and slammed the metal door behind them. The two-way mirror vibrated from the shock. One detective flipped a chair around and sat across from George. His breath smelled of sausage. The other detective leaned against a corner of the room. He spoke first. "I'm Detective Triana and he's Detective Bailey. You look tired, George. You tired?"

"A little."

"Yeah. I can see why. Busy week. House decorating. Rounds of golf. Murdering your playing partner. Wear me the hell out so I can imagine how beat you are."

"It was an accident."

Bailey leaned over the table. "Accident my ass. What do we look like, George? Dumb shit rookies on our first case? You lie to us, you spend your last ten years of your life nuzzling lowlifes in Raiford." Bailey threw his hands up in mock disgust. Bad cop, bad cop. It wasn't like Law and Order. George tried to calm his heartbeat. Patience.

"All right, all right," Bailey said. "We got the cameras rolling, audio on. You are here voluntarily, right?"

"Yes."

"And you said you didn't want a lawyer so the floor is yours, George. Let's hear it right down to the part where you drown Dr. Peregrine in the muck."

"It was an accident."

"Mind if I smoke?" Triana said as he lit a cigarette.

"I can't see well." George took off his heavy glasses and waved them in front of Bailey. "I have macular degeneration. I thought I was driving to the green. I didn't see the pond. I'm sorry. I really am. When the cart flipped over I couldn't see Kathryn, but she must have been under it. I'm so sorry."

"So if your vision is that bad, why were you driving?" Bailey said.

"Kathryn—Dr. Peregrine was drinking and I'm not sure she could have handled the cart. I'm sure she couldn't have."

The detectives thought about that for a second. Good. He wanted them to question their own conclusions.

"Okay," Bailey said. "Let me tell you the whole story, George. We've had two days and made some goddamn startling discoveries. Especially in your apartment."

"Condo."

"Okay—condo. Here's how it went down. Sometime in the recent past you met the good doctor Kathryn G. Peregrine and decided you was gonna do a Hinckley. We checked, George, your bedroom looked like a shrine to the late doctor. Pictures of her all over your walls. Little hearts around her like something a school kid might draw for a sweetheart. So you keep a journal of love poems and oaths to your beloved and then sell your pension and RV so you can be with her at her private club. So, Georgie—you're nuts, but it ain't no crime to obsess. But then you had to go and kill her."

"I didn't."

"You killed her, but it wasn't because of all that crap, was it? You know why you did it, don't you George?"

"No, I don't."

"Yes, you do. You did it for Isabel."

George was silent for a few seconds, then said, "That's a lie."

Triana lit another cigarette. The smoke made George's vision worse. It was difficult to make out their faces.

"Two years ago, Isabel had surgery for a bad back, "Bailey said. " Not minor, either. Serious shit for a sixty year old. Risky stuff."

"I was there," George said. "We knew the possible outcomes. I don't need you to tell me what I already know."

"Testy, George. Calm down. A man headed for prison needs to preserve his energy, right? So anyways, coincidentally, Dr. Kathryn Peregrine is your wife's surgeon that day and coincidentally, she screws up the surgery, and then coincidentally, Isabel dies on the operating table. So what do you do? You wait. Take your time to exact your revenge. You're patient. Wait until everybody forgets about Isabel and then carry out your plan. Sell the farm and cozy up to the doc at the country club until you can get her alone and then off her. Pay her back for killing Isabel, right?"

"It wasn't Kathryn's fault. Isabel and I knew the risk."

"Yeah," Bailey said. "But you blamed her anyway. You must have thought we were morons not to figure it out. She kills Isabel, you kill her. There's your motive. Who the hell knows why you go to all that trouble with the pictures and diary shit, but what it comes down to is just good old vengeance. An eye for an eye."

George stood, startling the detectives. Both unsnapped their holsters at the same time. "I didn't kill her! It was an accident! I'm telling the truth. I loved Kathryn. I've loved her since before Isabel's surgery when Kathryn came into the waiting room and explained the procedure. I had never seen a more beautiful woman in my life. She loved me too, I could feel it. I could never kill her, I loved her. All I wanted was to be near her, to smell her, to touch her. In time, she would have felt the same about me. I know she would have. It was an accident. I wouldn't kill her. I loved her. I did. I loved her. I loved her..." George sobbed into his hands and then looked up at the detectives. Even with his poor vision, he saw a puzzled look on their faces, and then just a moment of doubt. That was all George wanted, a small amount of reasonable doubt. It was all he'd need from the jury.

J.J. WHITE

Dr. Adelman

Published 2009 Helium.com

"First—do no harm. That line is purported to be part of the Hippocratic Oath all doctors are required to take, although I can assure you, our protagonist, the esteemed Dr. Adelman, has no intention of keeping his oath.

You would guess it a test of your patience to read an almost three thousand word story about an elderly doctor struggling in the less than exciting milieu of Flatbush, New York, and you would be correct. I myself speed read over all but the interesting parts and so it only took a minute for this gem.

There is a rather instructive lesson on surgically removing a voice box from a pit bull that I found interesting, but except for that and the gratuitous violence the rest of the tale was sappy, emotional and clap-trap.

Skip it and go on to the next one."

~ G.R.

This would be the most important surgery of Dr. Mattias Adelman's sixty-year career as a physician. Mattias leaned over as far as his ninety-three-year old bones would let him and petted the three light brown American pit bull pups. One of the pups snapped at Mattias' thumb.

"Oh, you are what they say you are, my little friends. Such aggression from one so young, but it is not your fault of course. You are like them." He pointed out the smoky window of his Flatbush row house at three teenagers playing one on one at a net-less basketball hoop.

"And they are like you, no? Fierce and angry but ah—that was how they were bred, no? Like you, little pups, it is all they know."

Mattias walked slowly to the window to pull closed the curtains Helen had made with her own hands forty years ago. They had enough money at the time to buy a nice set of curtains but they had both grown up during the depression and were not able to change their thrifty ways regardless of their financial condition.

Before he could close the curtain, one of the three boys pointed to him. It was Antoine. Mattias knew their names. He knew quite a bit about each of the three. Marcus and Antoine both lived across the street in the large public housing project, raised by their grandmothers, like so many others. The white boy who hung out with them was called Beck. Mattias was unsure if it was short for a last name, maybe Beckham or Becker.

Antoine said something to the others and then casually dribbled the ball in the direction of Mattias' apartment. Mattias left the curtains open and stood steadfast in the window. He was too old and had seen too much to be intimidated by a bully.

Antoine stopped just short of the window and grinned. He pointed to a red gem embedded in his left incisor. Helen's. It was Helen's ruby, a chip from the larger stone. Antoine was flaunting his prize to Mattias.

Mattias closed the curtains and hummed Liebestraum to calm himself and drown out Antoine's laughter.

The puppies barked, first to one another and then to Mattias who waved a finger at them. "Oh no, no, my friends. I can't feed you now. It would be a waste of good milk, you see."

He went into the second bedroom he still used as an office, where the poor and the forgotten came to him for his help. How could he refuse now? He had not refused for sixty years and he would not start now. The sick had changed over the years from mostly white and Jewish to now mostly black and Hispanic but they were still his patients and he would do his best for them.

He stooped to pick up a black leather bag, the handle worn to a smooth shine, its leather sides creased from frequent opening and closing.

"Ah, my bag. Where would I be without you? You have served me well and never once complained. Yes, yes."

Mattias placed the bag on the stainless bed and opened it to survey its contents. He was looking for something specific and if it was like every other time he needed an item, it would be at the bottom. Such was life.

He removed some forceps and a packet of tongue depressors wrapped in waxy paper that had turned brown from age.

"Aha," he said and removed two hypodermic syringes, a scalpel and some blades.

Back in the living room, he placed the instruments on the floor near the three yapping pups. It took him several minutes but Mattias was able to retrieve a small white bottle from an upper cabinet. It was his last bottle of Propofol. Probably four or five years old but the anesthetic would work well enough for such a minor surgical procedure.

He would use the true surgical approach to the operation. No reason to do the work halfway. Halfway work, as he knew from experience, results in halfway results, and the consequences of a botched surgery were severe. He must succeed for Helen.

Mattias hadn't realized he was crying until he saw the tears near the bag. What was wrong with him? Helen would be ashamed of him showing such emotion while working. For shame.

He lifted the spotted pup and placed him gently on the stainless bed. The puppy squirmed in his hand.

"I will call you Moses since you want to flee so badly, my friend. Moses of Flatbush. Such an honor to serve your master, no?" He pointed to the other pups. "And you two will be Solomon and Joshua."

Mattias shoved the needle of the syringe into the bottle of Propofol. He grabbed Moses by the scruff of the neck and held him fast to the slippery table. Moses panted and smiled at his master. Perhaps he thought he'd receive one of those delicious treats Mattias fed him. "No, not this time, proud Moses. This will not hurt but for a few seconds."

Mattias poked the needle into the back of the dog's shoulder and pushed the plunger. Moses jerked for a few seconds and then flopped on his side like a fish. The other dogs yapped relentlessly at the old doctor as if they instinctively knew Moses had been hurt.

"Solomon, Joshua, when have I ever harmed you? Never, yes, you must not worry, little wise ones. Your friend will soon be awake and tormenting you as all good friends do, no? Patience, my boys. You are next."

Mattias turned his attention back to Moses who seemed to be dreaming something wonderful as his tongue slid back and forth in rhythm with his eyeballs as he chased an imaginary rabbit or mouse.

Mattias held the scalpel with the precision of a young, fearless surgeon and made an incision across Moses' neck. The happy pup made no movement as the Propofol induced an even wider smile from the happy dog.

The doctor's fingers flew through the surgery as they had for countless years at Mount Sinai saving lives of thousands or at least extending the lives of the sick and the helpless. Why couldn't he have used his skills on Helen as she lay there gasping for breath, her heart frantically trying to overcome the death squeeze of cardiac arrest? He could have saved her or prolonged her life, but he was at the hospital, saving those less deserving. Poor Helen.

Mattias spread the flesh of the neck until the cords were visible. Several cuts with the razor sharp scalpel until Mattias had removed all the dog's vocal cords. Now came the difficult part. He wished he had the assistance of another physician as he stitched the voice box open but he knew he could tell no one of his plan.

Mattias improvised with a hemostat, positioned to keep the voice box exposed. Twenty minutes later, he had finished and bandaged the puppy's neck with gauze. Poor Moses would be very sore for a few days but then would quickly recover enough to play with Solomon and Joshua. Soon, the first part of Mattias' yearlong plan would be complete.

He stared down at Moses who, though somewhat bloody, was still smiling.

"Dear God, forgive me." Mattias pressed his hands together and wondered how he would explain to Helen's spirit what he was up to before he fell asleep later.

A year later, Mattias was still in good health despite his age and crooked back. Each day after the final patient had left his office he would carry a pail of meat out to the fenced-in patio of his house where he kept the dogs caged.

By early evening the dogs were famished and in near frenzy to eat. Today he had only chicken to feed to the boys, but when the opportunity arose at the hospital morgue, Mattias would furtively remove an appendage from a transient or a John Doe to sate the hunger of the pit bulls. On those occasions, he would pull the bolt from the cage and fling the arm or leg into the small grassy area behind the porch. Moses, Solomon and Joshua would clamp on the dismembered appendage and violently rip the flesh in their canine tug-of-war.

It was cruel to starve the dogs and a sin to slice a cadaver to feed his boys, but necessary to achieve the results he hoped for.

He walked over to the porch and hooked three chickens on ropes that hung from the ceiling of the porch. He released the bolt from the cage. The dogs patiently watched the swinging chickens until Mattias yelled in Hebrew, *"Beezras Hashem!"* The dogs sprinted to the ropes, jumped high, clamped their viselike jaws on the chickens, and swung like hangmen until Mattias gave them a signal. Then the dogs shook the meat off the hooks, fell expertly to the ground, and flew back to the cage to eat.

Satisfied, Mattias went back in the apartment to read. In a week, he thought, they would be over a year old and ready. It was time.

"Eat well, boys," Mattias said softly to himself. "It is all you will eat for a week."

Saturday, the delivery trucks came. Mattias specifically asked that everything be delivered between 8 and 9 a.m., the time when Antoine and his friends shot hoops.

The men unloaded the 52" plasma TV. Not cheap, perhaps as much as he had ever paid for a single item before. The last time he had spent that much money was on a new car for Helen. That was years ago. How wonderful her expression when he surprised her.

The three teenagers froze mid-game and watched intently as the deliverymen unloaded the TV, a surround sound system, and finally, expensive video games. Antoine grinned. Helen's ruby glistened in the morning sun.

Mattias tipped the men a few dollars. They seemed disappointed with the few bills Mattias handed to them. How things have changed. So many want so much more than they deserve.

And now he had only to wait as he understood human nature and greed made one do stupid things. Perhaps he would be wrong. Perhaps his plan would fail but he thought not. Predictability was a given when it came to thieves. Thieves and murderers.

Mattias opened the door to the guest bedroom and surveyed the scene. The boxes of new electronic equipment lay in the corner of the room unopened, as they would remain. He had the receipts to return them later. He reached over the lamp table, pulled the latch open on the dog cage and hurriedly backed out of the room, shutting the door behind him.

He paused at Helen's portrait in the hallway. He had it commissioned twenty years ago. Her wrinkles and gray hair couldn't mask her overwhelming beauty. She had been lovely. Too good for an old doctor, God knows.

Mattias pulled the portrait off the wall and set it next to him on the side of the old rocker, and waited. He didn't have to wait long. The noise came from the porch door.

First a cutting, scraping sound, then a large crack and the shattering of glass. Antoine and his friends had arrived. Mattias said nothing. The one called Beck peeked around the corner of the hallway and stared at him. Mattias held the tough boy's gaze and continued to rock in the chair.

All three teenagers walked into the great room and stood towering over Mattias. Only Beck had a gun. He raised it level with Mattias' head and chambered a round. Mattias knew the weapon. He didn't live in a shell. It was a .40 caliber semi-automatic pistol with a fifteen shot magazine. He flinched when Beck placed the muzzle against his forehead.

Antoine chuckled. "What do you need all that shit for old man?"

Mattias said nothing.

"I asked you a question, Aldelman."

Mattias remained silent.

"Now where is it?"

No answer.

Antoine gestured to Beck. "If this old man don't talk in the next five seconds, you bust him with that .4, hear me? One—two—three—four . . ."

"It's in the guest bedroom," Mattias said in a flat tone. He was glad his voice had shown no sign of fear. Bullies, that's all they were. Bullies and killers.

"Watch him," Antoine ordered as he and Marcus went into the bedroom. "Shit!" came Antoine's muffled exclamation.

"All there?" Beck asked.

"Hell, yes," Antoine replied.

Mattias yelled out, *"Beezras Hashem!"*

Antoine and Marcus screamed. The unmistakable sound of an attack, the shouts of surprise, the cries for help, transformed into gurgling, muffled pleas as the din quieted to the efficiency of ripped flesh and splayed blood.

Beck yelled out to Antoine, turned back to Mattais, hesitated, and then ran to rescue his accomplices. Soon after he entered the bedroom his own screams were drowned out by the report of the one shot and then another.

Mattias stood from the rocker, walked to the bedroom and shut the door. He slipped into his jacket, placed his fedora on his head and walked out the front door of his house with the aid of the cane Helen gave him on their sixty-fifth anniversary.

He walked three blocks and knocked on the apartment door of his good friend Morey Weinstein. Morey took his time, but finally opened the door. He was also dressed in a jacket and tie and had a hat under his arm.

"Oh ,God, it must be the end of the world. Are we being invaded? The big shot Dr. Aldelman knocks on my door for only the second time this century. Someone call the rabbi, for I must be dead."

"You were always the smart ass, Morey," Mattias said. He walked by Morey and sat down in a large recliner in the living room.

"Sit down, make yourself at home," Morey said. "And to what do I owe this honor?"

Mattias removed his hat and placed it by the cane. "How long have we been friends?"

"Never, friends," Morey said. "I suffered your acquaintance for eighty years now, you shlimazel."

"Yes—and I yours, you putz, but I still call you friend and I have a favor to ask of you."

"Mattias, you have more money than Trump. I should ask you for favors. I eat cat food three times a day."

"Your cat should be so lucky. Seriously, old friend. I need help."

Morey sat on the couch and removed his hat. "I'm late for temple."

"It can wait."

"Yes—it can. For you Mattias, the answer is, I will do anything at all. You know that without asking. Now, what is it? Did you get a girl pregnant?"

Mattias smiled. "I need you to call the police and tell them you went by my house on the way to temple and saw three hoodlums breaking into the back."

"Why?"

"I don't want you to ask why."

"Why don't you want me to ask why?"

"Because I don't."

Morey sighed and shook his head. "My father was a cop."

"I know."

"My brother was a cop."

"I know."

"Well—then you know I will not lie to a cop. You know that, my friend, and on a Saturday, too."

"I'm sorry," Mattias said.

"You're sorry. What have you done?"

"I can't say."

"You know I would do anything for you, but that."

"Yes, I know."

Morey stared into Mattias' eyes. "Does this have something to do with those boys and Helen?"

Mattias nodded. His eyes welled with tears.

"Are they the same ones?"

Again, he nodded.

"Okay, I'll do it, but not for you. I'll do it for Helen."

Mattias grinned sadly and held out his hand. Morey took it.

"Besides, I was once in love with Helen. She was the best looking of all the girls. I asked her to marry me in '33."

Mattias sat back in the recliner. "So, you tried to steal my girl from me, Morris Weinstein."

"I did but she said she would rather marry an ugly doctor than a good looking banker."

"Lucky me," Mattias said.

"Yes. Lucky you, you putz." Morey squeezed Mattias' hand. The two men stood." You know, Matty. Helen was something special."

Mattias hugged Morey and rested his head on his old friend's shoulder. His tears stained the jacket.

"Yes, she was, my friend."

Tour Bus

First Place, Flash Fiction, Grey Sparrow *Fiction Competition, 2012*

Published, Grey Sparrow Journal, 2012

Nominated for Pushcart Prize, *2013*

"This repetitive and interminable piece of flash fiction follows no traditional style of writing I can recall. Perhaps the author wrote it while sleeping, or dreaming, or shrooming. Who can tell? The writing borders on abuse of the elderly, the one redeeming quality of the narration in my opinion.

I see this was nominated for the Pushcart Prize. Apparently the criteria for literary awards these days are not as severe as they used to be.

A dog dies. It's worth reading for that."

~ *G.R.*

Consider a tour bus full of senior citizens working its way through a congested Washington D.C. street, but no, the street is actually the North Yungas Road in Bolivia, and there's no room to spare as the wheels hang perilously over the edge while the occupants rush one side to view the magnificent rainforest below, but no, they scream for the driver to stop the bus and let them out and the bus driver understands English and stops the bus, but no, he knows no English and keeps going, the road narrowing as they ascend the mountain until a police car blocks their progress and flags the bus to a stop, but no, a small truck edges between the bus and the sheer rock wall, forcing the bus and its hapless occupants over the edge and down the embankment, the bus stopping its death slide after a few feet, stuck securely by huge boulders, but no, it topples hundreds of feet to the bottom, gray-haired passengers thrown out broken windows to their death and hours later, rescuers remove the survivors, including Claire and her shih-tzu, Penny, but no, Bolivian agents kidnap the injured Claire and deliver her to the secret police where the interrogator complains to his colonel that he cannot torture an old woman, but no, the man screams for Claire to tell him where it is, the blade of his small knife working its way up her fingernail, yet she refuses to answer and kicks at him, but no, she begs him to stop as the torturer pours gasoline on her beloved Penny and holds a lighter over the beast while Claire crumbles, whimpering, revealing everything, but no, she stands fast, silently watching her dog explode in a conflagration of fur and flesh, and Claire sobs, hours later, blindfolded, bound, and laid across the transmission hump of an old truck or car, she feels weightless as the vehicle falls hundreds of feet down a hill, her body thrown violently against the interior, but no, she slides effortlessly into the bus seat next to a young man who looks like her father had looked when he was that age and fought in the great war.

J.J. WHITE

The Murderous Mr. Pip

Finalist in the 2009 "Scare the Dickens Out of Me"
Short Story Competition

"It is 1940, and on a cold December day, Adolph Hitler's Luftwaffe is devastating London with its relentless bombing of centuries-old buildings, leaving thousands dead in their wake.

Let me stop here and say something about Hitler. Never has one person been more responsible for the deaths of so many innocent than the leader of the Third Reich. Singlehandedly he sent millions to their graves. A monster. A miscreant, void of morals, void of conscience, void of mercy.

What a man.

Back to our story.

Phillip Pirrip IV's duties as a Home Guard volunteer are to identify and count these bombers as they fly over Kent toward London. Phillip, known as Pip, by his lovely wife, Millie, is a descendant of Phillip Pirrip I, he also known as Pip in Dickens' Great Expectations. If you read your classics I wouldn't have to explain.

An unexploded fifty kilogram bomb accidentally falls in Phillip's backyard giving him an idea that could not only save his beloved Satis House that he inherited, but also rid him of his nagging fat wife. Using all his engineering skill, he rigs the bomb to explode when Millie enters the great dining room.

Mortality is close. I wait, scythe in hand. Will Phillip succeed? Ah, there's the conundrum. Whether he does or not he certainly gets more than he bargained for."

~ *G.R.*

Kent, England – December 23, 1940

Philip Pirrip IV tried furiously to keep a respectable count of German bombers as they flew over him and the Kent coast on their way to blitz London or perhaps Manchester.

Each time he looked up into the gray skies, his Home Guard helmet slid a little more on the back of his head. Finally, he'd had enough of the bloody thing, unloosed the chinstrap, and let it fall to his backyard.

He'd lost count. Best to improvise. With six bombers abreast and three large formations of five rows he ciphered about a hundred so far. They'd rip the living hell out of London as they had since September. That he knew for sure.

As he sighted another formation just coming into view, he saw a black object fall out of one of the bombers. A man perhaps, but why would Fritz jump out of a perfectly able craft?

"Bloody hell," he said aloud as the black dot grew larger on its free-fall towards—well, towards him, it seemed. It traveled fast and if it indeed was a man, the bloody idiot best open his chute soon or he'd fall to a certain death, all right, and might just take Philip with him.

Philip dodged to the left and the object seemed to follow. It was nearly on him and he knew he should run for shelter, but continued his fixed gaze, mesmerized by its progress.

It was but a few seconds from impact when Philip realized what it was. A bomb. A bomb and in a few seconds he would be dead, blown apart because of his damn curiosity.

It did not hit Philip, but nearly did so. He fell to the ground as he had been trained by the military and was flipped on his back by the concussion. He had no time for regrets, not even enough to make peace with a God he was not sure he believed in.

There was a strange silence as Philip stared up at the fast moving clouds. The bombers were gone. He turned his head left, then right, and then patted his head, chest and legs. He seemed to be all there.

Why hadn't he blown up with the bomb? He stood, brushed off a good deal of dirt, and walked over to a crater the size of a man. In it was a green bomb, perhaps 50 kilograms, its red fins mangled by the impact. A dud. It must have fallen out of a bomber by accident. It would be no real coup for Hitler to bomb a dilapidated house of an engineer in Kent,

---

Author's Note: "Philip Pirrip IV" is a descendant of the character "Pip" from Charles Dickens's novel, *Great Expectations* (1861).

for God's sake, even a large structure the size of Satis House, his inheritance from his father, Philip Pirrip III.

It must have been an accident, then. Some Jerry had erred and let loose a bomb early. Lucky for Philip the trigger had not gone off, probably because it was not armed. It was difficult to think a German airman could be so careless when they supposedly take so much pride in their morbid efficiency.

Philip looked around. It seemed that no one other than him had seen the missile fall into his backyard. Millie was at her sister's in London. With a bit of luck, one of Jerry's armed bombs would find her well. Not likely though. Adolph wouldn't dare risk an attack on the formidable Millie Pirrip. If the explosion didn't kill her she'd hunt Hitler down and nag him to death as she surely would Philip before the war had ended.

It was at that distasteful moment in thought that Philip concocted his dastardly plan. Was it possible? Could he actually take advantage of this act of providence and finally rid him of his adversary, his foe, his nemesis, his daughter of Satan, his beloved bride of twenty years? Yes—he could.

He knew this bomb. He knew everything about it, its size, how it functions, its enormous capability for destruction. He could do it and he would. But he would have to act fast. Millie would be home soon after the blitz in London, being so near Christmas.

There was little time to waste. First, he must dig the device out of his backyard. The two hundred kilometer per hour velocity of the projectile impaled it a good five feet into his soggy yard.

Philip rushed to the gardening shed to retrieve a shovel. The shed was all that was left of a brewery owned by the first Philip Pirrip. It, along with the Satis House, was property willed to his wife Estella by the mysterious Miss Havisham, the original owner. The house was now a shambles from years of neglect. Philip made little income from his engineer's job and saw no need to waste what wages he made on the enormous ancient structure.

Ah—but the bomb and his plan would solve that little problem. Philip may have had small wages and no savings, but he did have a life assurance policy on his beloved Millie that would be worth a bit more than the Satis House was worth.

He dug quickly but carefully to clear the dirt and muck from around the bomb. Yes, it was a 50 kilogram as he had thought. A Sprenbombe SC type with an ECR 15 electrical fuse. He knew of the bomb and many others like it. He felt it was his duty to England and the King to know everything about every piece of armament the Jerrys could fling at them.

It was nearly ten p.m. when Philip finally secured the bomb with chains that were attached to a two-meter tri-pod he and his brother used for lifting engines out of automobiles. Roger had quizzed Philip on the need to borrow the contraption, but Philip successfully fended off his brother's curiosity by making up some excuse about removing old stumps.

Philip cranked the handle of the tripod and a half hour later, the bomb swung heavily above the hole. There was still enough sunlight in the winter evening to haul his prize into the house.

Using a dolly, Philip carefully pulled the bomb up the front steps, through the back door and into the hallway separating the storage room from the kitchen.

He was exhausted, but after a short break, pulled the dolly and its heavy load up the fifteen steps and into the great dining room with its four-meter length ebony table and giant fireplace. The room was filled with thick dust that covered great stained glass windows and choked Philip's throat. He placed the bomb underneath the majestic dining table.

That was enough for the night. He was too spent to continue further. The great plan would continue in the morning. He would have more than enough time to fill the crater out back and set the trap for Millie. It was time for bed. Time for sleep and dreams of a pleasant future.

The next morning, the telephone woke Philip. It was Millie. She would leave London that day and arrive in Rochester station early that evening.

"And why didn't you come to London to check on me, sir? Do you not care a fig about your wife to even see if she's alive or dead?"

Ah, but if only you were dead, Philip thought to himself.

Millie had been a looker when they first met, a fine looker. The sort of bird men fancied to look at and be with. A fine figure of a woman.

He so much adored that figure he ignored her shortcomings, a slight cockney brogue and a passion for food. Now the gluttony had done its work as the once svelte maiden now waddled like an emperor penguin. He probably could still tolerate her if she hadn't perfected the art of the nag. How could the Nazis pinpoint a bomb on top of a tiny Spitfire and not hit a woman the size of a house?

"I expect you'll have dinner when I arrive home, Pip, and I don't fancy cheese sandwiches, either. 'Ow you can be an engineer and not provide for 'ouse and 'ome is beyond me, I tell you."

"You know I don't like to be called Pip, Millie. My name is Philip."

"Aaowww! Excuse me yer 'ighness. I forgot your royal blood, I did. Just pick me up at the station and have a dinner with some meat in it. Is that so 'ard—Pip!"

Philip hung up on her. He'd have something for her all right. He'd give her a nice present for Christmas of the 50-kilogram type. Call him Pip, will she. He hated the nickname. It made him feel below his station in life.

Pick her up, indeed. Doesn't she know there's a war on? Waste what little ration of petrol they had on a trip to the station. She should bicycle like everyone else except for the strain it would put on the poor two-wheeler.

But enough of that. He was wasting time needed to prepare. He fetched his small compass saw and carefully climbed a long ladder to the roof of the Satis House. In an area above the old dining room, Philip loosed several slate tiles and cut a hole in the roof the approximate diameter of the bomb. He peered through to see sawdust on top of the old table. Perfect.

After negotiating the climb down the gothic structure to the safety of the ground, he hurried to the kitchen with a coil of eighteen gauge electrical wire. He spliced the wire to a spare car battery and push button circuit that he had installed in a cabinet earlier. From there he ran the wire under the carpet up the stairs, into the dining hall and over to the bomb. Then he ever so carefully removed the ECR 15 fuse out of the bomb. Mustering all of his engineering skill, he attached the wire to the fuse and placed it back in the bomb.

When Millie was in position later, Philip would make the electrical circuit up to the fuse with a push of a button.

Naturally, he would have to remove the wire before the army came to investigate the explosion. Hopefully there would be enough roof left to determine where the projectile penetrated and destroyed the old dining hall and of course, Millie.

The ride from the train depot seemed endless. Millie blabbered nonstop about the bombing, and their last minute escape to the tube tunnel, and how upset she was at him for not coming to London after he knew perfectly well the Germans had bombed the city.

Philip tried to tune her out as she continued her belittling of him all through dinner. He thought she had tired herself out and would retire soon when she unfortunately looked out the kitchen window to the backyard.

"What's that now?"

"What?" Philip said.

"That patch of dirt near my garden, that's what. What have you buried there? Something I should know about, Mr. Pip?"

Philip cringed at the name. Could he wait until the bombers returned or would he strangle her first? God knows.

"Cold must have killed it last week. I saw some snow in that area, I believe. Yesterday I dug it up and mixed a little seed is all. It's nothing."

"Nothing, Pip?" Millie said. "I'd say it's something when I go away to visit me sister for a few days and I come back to find my garden under attack. You leave the gardening to me and you worry about your machining and your Nazi bombers. You 'ear me?"

Philip mumbled something unintelligible.

"What's that Pip? Did you say something?"

"I said I heard you." And he did hear her. Hopefully not for much longer though if the German manufacturers are as good as they say.

On Christmas day, Philip watched, listened and waited for the hoped bombers and their lethal cargo destined for London. It was cruel of him to hope for something so ghastly and malevolent on a holiday, but he so desperately wanted to be rid of Millie.

Then the drone of the engines floated on the air, across the marshes and the villages to Satis House, and to the gleeful ears of Philip.

"Millie! Millie! Come quick!" He wondered if she could hear him over the noise of the bombers?

"Millie!"

"What?" Millie said, the contempt evident in her voice. She held the backdoor open.

"Go and fetch my posters, quickly!" exclaimed Philip. "In the hall. I'll need them to identify the class. Now quickly!"

"Fetch yer own damn posters."

"Millie, please!"

"Oh all right, but it's the last time—'ear?" She turned and shut the door.

Philip looked up to see the last formation of bombers overhead. He needed to hurry. He opened the backdoor and furtively made his way to the kitchen. Millie slowly worked her way up the stairs. When the squeaks of the old staircase ceased, Philip would count to five to allow enough time for his large wife to waddle to the door of the dining hall. Then he'd push the button to detonate the bomb.

He opened the first cupboard on the left, moved a ceramic vase away from the button and waited. The squeaks stopped. He counted. One—two—three—four—five.

There was a long silence. Philip held his breath. He was about to question his handiwork when the blast shook the house, the shockwave knocking him to the ground. He instinctively covered his ears, but it was too late as he felt his eardrums might burst from the ringing.

Bits of plaster fell from the kitchen ceiling onto his face and clothes. Philip gathered himself enough to stand and brush off.

The blast was not nearly as large as he thought it might be. Perhaps the neighbors hadn't even heard the explosion. If that were the case he would have to ring the police to inform them a bomb landed on his house and killed his wife.

"Look sir," he'd say. "It came in right there and left that hole." The constable would agree and then they'd find the poor Mrs. Pirrip under the debris—quite dead.

First, though, Philip would have to go upstairs to make sure that was true. He stepped over debris on the staircase. The last two steps had collapsed so he had to jump across the gap to the dust-filled hallway. The door to the room lay there, blown out from the blast. He stepped over it into the great dining room, no longer so great. The hole in the roof had disappeared along with a portion of the roof itself. The dining table had disintegrated. Only a few chairs had survived the blast.

Where was Millie? Had she disintegrated also? He nearly fainted when he heard a woman's voice behind him.

"Pip."

Surely she couldn't have lived through the destruction. How could God treat him so cruelly?

"Pip," the faint voice again said.

It came from the fireplace. He tentatively moved some busted wood pieces away from the hearth and bent down to peer up inside the flue.

"Aaaayeeee!" The high pitched shrill startled Philip knocking him back to the floor. A long streak of white mist flew from the fireplace and danced about the room at tremendous speed, darting from wall to wall, a luminous apparition that took no shape yet screamed that awful sound, "Aaaayeeee! Aaaayeeee!"

Philip covered his ears to no avail, the piercing screech tormenting him until he fell to his knees. "Stop—oh please, God—stop. It hurts so. Please I beg you—stop!"

It did. The apparition went silent and stopped directly in front of him. It metamorphosed into the translucent figure of a woman. She floated a meter or so above the debris that was once a grand table, her hair long and dirty grey, unkempt, yet her face beautiful, near angelic.

Philip's brain did not want to believe what his eyes saw but there it was. An apparition—a specter—a ghost. The ghost of a middle-aged woman, dressed in a worn, yellowed wedding gown, her feet shoeless and dangling like small church bells from the hem.

"Pip!" she screamed.

He couldn't speak. It was as if the air had been knocked from his lungs.

"Why?" she asked.

"Wh—why what?" he said, his voice cracking.

"Why have you called me back, Pip? Did you not finish what you had planned? Did you not get everything you wanted? The Satis House, the brewery, my Estella. Is there something more?"

"Who are you?" he asked.

She laughed for several seconds. "You don't remember your first benefactor. I, who helped you to leave the life of a smithy to enter a gentleman's world. Please tell me, Pip, you know the owner of the house you destroyed."

"Miss—Havisham?"

"The one," she said.

"Am I dead?" Philip asked.

"Not yet, but there's plenty of time for that, my dear. First, Pip, I expect an apology for my murder. You have come to apologize, have you not?"

The specter drew closer to Philip. He outstretched his arm to touch her. His hand passed through as if it were smoke.

"But no, you're confused, Miss Havisham. I'm not Pip."

She laughed again. "Oh, but you certainly look like Pip and you're living in Pip's house and I believe you murdered that woman over there who also called you Pip." She pointed to the old oak door.

"Well, yes, my name is Pip. Actually Philip Pirrip IV. You see, you think I'm the first Pip, my great grandfather who married Estella and inherited this house. That was in 1840. This is 1940. One hundred years later. You have me confused."

Miss Havisham flew in a circle around Philip, her eyes never leaving his. "And you wish me to take the word of a murderer. Tch-tch, Mr. Pip. You are supposed to be a gentleman. Now, apologize."

"But I am not—"

"Apologize!"

"For something I have not done? Apologize for what?"

"For this!" She screamed and turned her back to him. The scorched flesh dripped off her bones to the dusty floors. Maggots fed on her exposed brain through a black hole in her skull. The insects swept across the bloody matter like a white cloud. Philip heard a guttural scream, looked for its originator, and then realized it had come from him. He backed away from Miss Havisham but the ghost followed.

"Look at what you did, Pip! You let me burn!" She turned and pointed a bony finger at him. "You murdered me to get my house, my land, my Estella! You!"

"No—no!" Philip screamed. "I'm not Pip! Please! No!"

Miss Havisham rose to the opening in the roof, hovered for a moment, then flew down, down, towards the horrified engineer, her face blood red, eyes full of death.

* * *

The police sergeant lifted a lion's claw table leg from the floor and chucked it across the room. "Definitely a Jerry bomb, I'd say," he said to the shorter corporal. "Yes, not a large one, though. I'd say a hundred kilo, perhaps. Unlucky they were, to be the only recipient in all of Kent to be bombarded by the Nazis. Unlucky."

"Yes, quite," the corporal agreed. "Unlucky."

"Yes, quite," the sergeant repeated.

There was a faint moan from the front area of the bombed out room.

"Hello—what's that?" the corporal said. "Sounds like it's coming from under that door, sir."

The police sergeant and corporal lifted the door to see Millie staring up at them. They threw the door to the side.

"It's Mrs. Pirrip, sir," the corporal said. "Are you alright, madam?"

Millie sat up. She wiped some blood from her nose with the back of her hand and looked at it. "Oh God. Where am I? What the 'ell 'appened?"

The policemen helped her stand.

"A German bomb, madam," the sergeant said. "A direct hit, I'm afraid. A lot of damage to the house as you see. We thought you had perished. Thank God for that door. It probably saved your life."

"Yes—yes, now I remember. Pip sent me up 'ere for some charts or posters or something. I remember now."

"Mr. Pirrip?" the corporal asked.

"Yes, Mr. Pirrip asked me to fetch the bloody things. I remember opening the door 'alfway and then stopped when I saw a hole in the roof."

"Ah yes, madam," the sergeant said. "That would be from the bomb. Time delay fuse, I'm guessing. Clever lot those Germans."

"Pip," Millie said. "Where is Mr. Pip? Is he still in the yard?"

"I'm sorry, madam," the sergeant said. He pointed to a sheet draped body.

"Oh, God, my Pip," Millie cried. "Poor, poor Pip, and on Christmas, too." She walked over to the body. "I must see him, please. Once more afore they bury me husband, gentlemen."

"Mrs. Pirrip, that's not a good idea," the sergeant said. "Mr. Pirrip was—well it's just not a good idea."

"No, I won't 'ave it," she said and lifted the sheet. Philip's face was seared black, his eyeballs floating in the hollow sockets, staring up at Millie. She screamed and slumped into the sergeant's arms. A neighbor rushed into the room and helped Millie down the stairs.

"Wot do you suppose burned him like that, sir?" the corporal asked.

"The explosion of the bomb I gather," the sergeant replied.

"But sir. Why was he the only thing burned? You would think a fire big enough to do that damage to him would burn some of the room too, but there's no indication that anything else was set on fire. What do you suppose burned him?"

The sergeant rubbed his chin for a moment. "Friction, I'd say, corporal."

"Friction, sir?"

"At's right. I'd say it was a direct hit on this poor chap and the friction set him alit. Friction."

"Ah," the corporal said. "I suppose that's why you're the sergeant, sir."

J.J. WHITE

When Your Daddy Gets Home

Published 2009 Helium.com

"Melody Chance is not a very good mother. She neglects her children's basic needs of food and shelter. She's the type of mother you read about daily, the neglectful parent who says she loved her boy, as they wheel his body to the morgue.

What is the source of this behavior, you ask? I'll tell you since the author fails to, preferring the poor reader to figure it out. The source is Jesse, her husband, a man who rivals sweet Melody as a lousy parent.

But Melody's obsession has gone too far and only God or myself or Freud can help her now."

~ G.R.

Melody Chance shifted in the beach chair on their front lawn trying to scratch a pimple on her ass that had been bothering her for a week. With a cigarette in one hand, a Corona in the other, and no place on God's earth to put them, how the hell was she supposed to scratch the blessed thing?

"Loretta, hold these, baby." She handed the bottle and cig to her oldest, Loretta, a pretty seven-year-old with a smart mouth who should have been whipped more to make a decent child of her. Jesse never helped out when one of the brats needed whipping. She had to do it like it was Christ himself made the rules that women did the raising and men did whatever the hell their little brains and big dicks told them to do. Melody stood from the chair and scratched until it bled.

Twenty-six and she felt like fifty but who wouldn't after spitting out three human beings who no more cared about her than they would for some stranger who fed them, wiped their asses, and spent every extra cent on them when she herself could be enjoying that money on items that made her feel good. Melody's mother never spent money on her, she had to get it herself anyway she could and she did and she wasn't proud of it, but that's how she met Jesse and so maybe it wasn't such a bad thing after all.

Melody sat back down, shifting the bloody pimple between one of the green plastic slats. Her five-year-old, Hannah, stood from her miniature beach chair and reached for the Corona. A shadow from their neighbor's magnolia darkened the child's light blond hair, coloring it a burnt red like Jesse's. No doubt she was his, just like Loretta was and the three-year-old boy whose name Melody sometimes had trouble remembering.

"You sit your ass down, Hannah, and wait there for your daddy to get home or when he does I'll tell him you've been a bad girl and he'll whip your ass, you understand?"

Hannah sat, lowered her head and pushed aside small gray rocks with her toes until she could dig into the hard dirt. Jesse had the bright idea two years ago that he'd kill all the grass on the front lawn and replace it with white gravel. "Baby, we'll never have to mow no lawn no more, and I'll get me a few cacti . . ." He always tried to show he was smarter than she was by saying things like cacti instead of cactus, but she was not in the least impressed. "Yeah, a few cacti and some of them plants that don't need no water like they growed in Vegas and we'll have the prettiest front lawn in the neighborhood."

Well, it wasn't pretty. It was just butt-ass ugly and the rocks accumulate on the driveway when it rains and she ain't gonna sweep them up any more even when he complains it messes up the tires on the F-150 and who the hell cares, it's a pick-me-up truck, they're supposed to run over rock.

Melody nudged Loretta. "Baby, light me another. Can you do that?"

Loretta stood and nodded. "Yes ma'am." Loretta lifted the pack of Marlboro Lights and deftly smacked the pack four times into the palm of her left hand. On the last smack, she lowered her hand enough for two cigarettes to pop out an inch. She pulled one out, spun it between her index and middle finger, then popped the filter between her lips. Two sucks from the flame and smoke blew from her nostrils.

A large man, dressed in a red jogging suit that made him look like a giant walking strawberry, stopped his weird arm-swinging duck-walk to stare at Loretta.

"What the hell you looking at?" Melody said in a raspy whine.

"Nothing," he said and motored on like a cheap Christmas wind-up toy.

"Damn right nothing," Melody said, fetching the lit cig from Loretta who was a little reluctant to give it up. "My Jesse comes home, he'll give you some nothing." But the man was out of earshot and in his own stinking world. Melody turned her attention back to Loretta. "What you doing home anyway, Angel? Ain't you supposed to be in school or something?"

Loretta ground her feet below Jesse's gravel, dirt covering everything but the pink insides of her toes. She shook her head. "I don't go to school no more, Momma. I told 'em you home-school me now so I don't need their school no more." She reached for the half-empty Corona on the chair arm. Melody got to it first and chugged three swallows.

"I ain't homeschooling nobody. You, Hannah, and what's his name—"

"Billy," Loretta said.

"Billy—are all going to school. You ain't hanging around here all day. You're going back tomorrow."

"T'morrow's Saturday."

"Don't you sass me, girl. You want 'T'morrow's Saturday' to be the last thing you hear on God's earth, then you just go ahead and say it again."

"Yes, ma'am."

"What?"

"No, ma'am."

"Damn right, no ma'am. Now sit and wait for your daddy."

But Jesse probably wouldn't be home for a long time, being Friday night when he likes to stop at that Irish pub after roofing all day, his muscles taut and brown, some one-toothed bitch hanging on his arm like she had any right to it.

More likely, he'd stumble in about ten, stinking of sweat and smelling like women but Melody didn't care. She liked him best when he stunk and squeezed her titties with his roof tile laying hands, rolling her nipple between his sandpapery index finger and thumb, his full weight on her, pounding rhythmically into their $600 Rooms-To-Go four-poster until the youngest wakes up crying from all the noise.

Melody sniffed the air.

"What smells like shit?" She looked over to Hannah, who had her head down. "Hannah, did you shit in your panties again? How old are you girl?" Hannah held up five fingers. "Well you get your ass inside with your sister and clean them damn things out." Melody turned to Loretta. "You do as I showed you, girl. Dump the turds in the bowl and flush, then when it's clean water, you rub them panties together till they're just yellow and hang em up to dry. You remember?"

"Yes, ma'am," Loretta said, then walked Hannah into the light pink cement block house.

Melody took a long drag on the cigarette and tried to figure out what time it was by the setting sun behind the Postlewait's house. Maybe six thirty or quarter to seven. Jessie would be on his third Southern Comfort on rocks and wondering whether the tits on that mousy little thing next to him were real or not. He denied his indiscretions, saying, "I don't need none of that strange sugar when I can get all the cootchie I needs right here at home and not have to pay a penny for it, no how."

She didn't care. She needed him now. Soon as he came stumbling in she was gonna shut them brats up somewhere and spend some of that me time with him until he forgets he's drunk and holds her like there's no tomorrow.

Loretta walked Hannah back to her chair. Hannah tucked her skirt between her legs and sat.

"She ain't got no more clean underwear," Loretta said, "so I gave her some of mine. Oh—and Billy's in the swimming pool."

Melody sipped the last of the Corona and nodded. "Well, that's industrial of you, Angel. You're a better momma than your momma. How old's that boy?"

"Three, ma'am."

"Can he swim?"

"I think so. The water's real dirty so I could only see the top of him, but it looks like he's moving pretty good—for a boy."

Melody blew out some smoke and tried to figure out what kind of tree that was at the P.J. Simpkin's house. She guessed dogwood, with its pretty white blossoms, but it was so damn big. She pointed her Marlboro Light at Loretta.

"He'll probably drown and the papers will come out with my picture and say, oh God, what a lousy mother to ignore her child and let him drown in their old pool and how could she do that. You know what I'm gonna have to do if that boy drowns?"

"No, ma'am."

"He drowns, I'm gonna have to drown you and poopy pants here because then I can say the devil spoke to me, that I heard voices that said to drown my poor little innocent children and they will all say I'm crazy and put me in a loony bin for a few months and then me and your daddy can go back to having some fun."

"I'm hungry," Loretta said.

"There's some of that cereal you had this morning in the kitchen."

"That's popcorn, not cereal."

"Well, you put some milk on it, Miss Prissy Pants, and it's just as good for you."

Loretta rubbed her stomach. Hannah rubbed hers too but probably just to copy her smart mouth sister. Billy came stumbling out the backyard toward them, wet as a dog, water sloshing in his diaper.

"Well, he ain't drownt, I guess," Melody said. "Go towel him off 'fore he freezes," she said to Loretta. Loretta walked Billy to the house like she had Hannah. When she came back, she had a dry Billy, clad only in underwear, and a bowl, half-full of popcorn. The three children ate handfuls at a time, leaving nothing for Melody, just like they always did, and just like her momma always did.

Melody lifted her arm over her head and smelled her pit. It was rank and Jesse could be home anytime. She picked Billy up and sat him in her chair.

"Loretta, I am gonna take a shower before your daddy gets home. You sit here and watch them and don't let the boy get back in the pool, hear?"

"Yes, ma'am."

"If your daddy comes home, you come and get me quick. You know how he likes his dinner soon as his feet hit the floor. Now you understand?"

Loretta swallowed the last four kernels of the popcorn and nodded.

"Yes, ma'am. I'll come and get you right away."

"That's good. You do that," Melody said as she disappeared behind a screen door that had no screen.

* * *

Billy slipped out of his mamma's chair and climbed into Loretta's lap, shivering. Loretta pulled him close to her and covered his chest with her arms. Mrs. Wilson came out her front door from across the street with her dog, Buster, on a leash. Loretta would like a dog like it or maybe one a little bigger that could run and keep up with her. When she was older, she'd move out with Hannah and Billy into a big house and they'd share her dog. Mrs. Wilson and Buster walked over to them. Buster sniffed at Hannah, who pulled her legs up on the seat of the chair.

"Good evening, children," Mrs. Wilson said.

"Good evening, Miz Wilson," Loretta replied for the three of them.

"Where's your momma, darlin'?"

"She's inside taking a shower, Miz Wilson. She's gettin' ready for when Daddy gets home."

Mrs. Wilson raised her eyebrows and didn't say nothing for a little bit.

"But, sugar. Your daddy's been dead 'bout a year now."

Loretta nodded. "I know that, Miz Wilson. But Momma, she forgets sometimes."

"I see," Mrs. Wilson said. Then she rubbed Billy's hair for some reason.

"Well, dear. You come over later and I'll give you some of those deviled ham sandwiches you like, you hear?"

"Yes, ma'am."

Hannah slipped off the chair and tiptoed around Buster to get to Loretta. She whispered in her big sister's ear. Loretta smiled at Mrs. Wilson.

"Hannah wants peanut butter."

"And jelly?" Mrs. Wilson asked Hannah.

Hannah just nodded.

Muse Janice

Second Place Fiction, 2009 Prescott Arizona Professional Writers Competition
Honorable Mention, 2009 CNW/FFWA Florida State Writing Competition

"This is another odd and experimental piece that, regardless of its content, fits the criteria for Death's Twisted Tales. A twist and a death.

That a girl could be a muse is rather interesting except that if one has a muse, wouldn't one also have a talent that needed urging on by this muse? One would think so but not in this case.

I expect this is a fantasy of the author and not a piece garnished from reality. To summarize: A girl dies. A boy pines."

~ G.R.

Do you know Janice Geary?" my mother asked.

I did.

Janice made life tolerable in my intolerable world that without her, just occupied space, pushing, separating, defining life from an existence left void of anything that otherwise might be interesting.

She jumped up on the Mr.-Lau's-third-period-science-class-wobbly-twenty-year-old-at least-desk, with its inkwell holes and jackknife etched love oaths of graduated students who, like us, were never taught science or math or any other subject by Mr. Lau—because—because—because he was black and he'd say, you white kids never get black history, well you'll get it from me and we did.

And Janice—sweet muse Janice, kicking barefoot, wonderfully balanced on top of the love oath etched desk top—singing a cappella—Jagger style, Satisfaction, as if she were the only one in the room, trancelike, zombielike, flirtatious and gyrating to the imaginary band. "I can't get no—I can't get no—satisfaction."

But it didn't matter how off key or inane the surreal dance-song was. I watched enthralled, entranced, sexually stimulated by the gyrations, the translucent mesh blouse revealing perfect breasts as they swayed opposite her intentions. Body left—breasts right—body right—breasts left.

My dreams exposed, my fantasy of the asphalt black bottoms of her feet playfully entangled with mine. A dream, a wanton hope of a boy who feared fear, feared chance, feared life, but desired Janice, who cared nothing of the destination, but lived for the ride, baby!

"Yeah, I think she's in one of my classes," I replied to my mother, knowing anytime she asked me if I knew someone, something bad must have happened to them. Mom was an ER nurse who lived to describe the previous night's excitement. I knew then that Janice was dead, or hurt, or under arrest—the only three things that ever happened to wild girls in our neighborhood.

Janice's dance resumed, halted only by a pause to smile at me, like a master smiles at her new puppy, my wide eyes gazing in utter adoration for the all-knowing god of an owner and Janice knew—oh she knew the look I gave her, and she would think—You may want me, boy, but it'll never happen in this lifetime because there's so much more in this world than just your puppy dog eyes to latch onto.

She belted out the song, "When I'm drivin' in my car—and that man came on the radio . . ." and we all felt it now, the whole class moved by her intensity, the wobbly metal legs of the desk straining under her weight, ready to buckle—saved by the black six-foot-four Mr. Lau, presenting his hand to Janice like she was the queen herself, helping her off the desk that other girls would comment on later as having showcased the redneck chick when she made a spectacle of herself, but I didn't care.

She stepped down and brushed my face with the see through gauze blouse intentionally, no, maybe not intentionally, but later, alone, at night, in the dark, I would recall it as intentionally.

She frowned at Mr. Lau, the uppity Negro, as she'd say later about how some uppity Negroes just didn't know how to have fun and only wanted to talk about black history in science class that nobody remembers anyway. Well—maybe Crispus Attucks or Malcolm X would be indelibly etched in our minds when we were old and boredom caressed us like an afternoon stripper.

My mother continued. "They came in about three this morning, her, Gene Patterson and Billy Hale. The boys were okay."

That meant Janice wasn't, but I knew that earlier by the way my mother had asked if I knew Janice.

The impromptu song over, the impromptu dance interrupted, replaced with placid, pleasing quiet in the double-wide plywood, Plexiglas, persimmon smelling, portable classroom, sheltering placid, pleasing us from the heat and rain and a world without Janice, no different than the world inside, where one as correct as I could never be with one so uncivilized, uncouth, unintelligible, unattainable, unworldly as her.

Mr. Lau opened the portable's door to—what? Let air in? Let air out? The butterfly flew high above his head, flitting up and down, left and right, drawn by the flames, the inferno, where the fun was, and where it would always be, to those that embrace the action and excitement that's inherently repelled by one's instincts she'd never experience. It flitted until it didn't, and landed in the center of the universe, too compelled by her charisma to escape.

Janice smashed it with the palm of her hand, wiped its guts on her jeans and drummed to an imaginary song on the desktop with the tips of her fingers.

"She was DOA," Mom continued. "She went half-way through the windshield when the car flipped. They were drunk, of course."

Of course, I thought.

"Her head must have hit the pavement and scraped along the road because her scalp was nearly pulled off her head. Did you know the boys?"

I nodded. "I know Gene."

She continued. "He's fine, so's Billy Hale. I don't know what kind of parent would let teenagers drive around at two o'clock in the morning. Did you say you knew her?"

"Some."

"Well—she's dead, now."

Not entirely—when there's left something, a remnant of existence left to pine, to dwell, to obsess on, like the outline of a block of wood on a driveway, it's silhouette frozen by the spray of a dollar thirty-nine black paint can or the indelible body imprint on a bachelor's mattress.

The butterfly was dead, but at least it flew.

Emily Wasn't There

Published 2011 Helium.com

"When one knows one's death is near, it's only natural the last thoughts would be of loved ones, whether a child or spouse, though one could be thinking of the idiots who put you into the life and death situation, like our protagonist in this odd tale. Often I creep up to the suffering and speed their untimely death to limit unnecessary pain, as I have in this case.

See, I'm not entirely evil. I still like bunnies—and dark chocolate—and little baby ducks."

~ G.R.

Her right arm was broken. Both feet were held fast by a large piece of metal. She couldn't feel her toes. Her feet were probably broken too. She bled from a wound in her right calf. Blood pulsed in sync with her heartbeat. The floorboard carpet shone pink in the dull light of the interior as the stain spread out in a circle. She hit the bent steering wheel where the horn should have been, but the only noise was the whoosh of powder escaping from the deflated airbag.

She couldn't tell if the wound was a laceration or a puncture. Either would kill her if enough blood drained from her body. Judging from the flow, it had to be a Class II hemorrhage. Her heart rate would soon increase rapidly and her blood pressure would drop.

The disadvantages and advantages of being a nurse. She had the disadvantage of knowing she was dying and the advantage of knowing how long she had to live. Not long at all from the look of the floorboard.

One headlight still shone on the sparse flora that survived in the dried up riverbed. A mist hovered below the illumination adding to the eerie scene. How far had the car fallen? A hundred feet? She had no idea, but it seemed to go on forever once she had driven over the edge.

It was Bill's fault. No. It was Jesse's fault.

The rearview mirror was relatively intact, just a small crack. She reached up with her left hand and focused it on the backseat. Emily wasn't there. The car seat wasn't there. Had she taken Emily with her? She was so faint she couldn't even remember her own name. It was short. Four letters. Lara or Kara or Jane.

She had been upset and had driven away. She was angry with Bill. No, she was pissed off at him. He called her a whore. Does sleeping with another man make you a whore? What do they call a man when he sleeps with another woman?

The windshield was translucent or transparent. What was the difference between the two? The safety glass had fractured when the car slammed into the large boulder. She could see the light from the one headlight and fuzzy images of rocks and the smashed front end and something else. Something moving.

"Help," she said, softer than she had intended. "Help me, please. I can't move and I'm bleeding." Whoever it was moved in front of what was left of the hood, blurry in the darkness outside the beam of light. And the light was dimming. Something was draining the battery.

Where was her cell phone? What time was it? The radio clock illuminated, though dimly. 3:32 a.m. No one would be on the highway. No one would see the dust on the auxiliary road she had accidentally turned on to, thinking of Bill and Jesse instead of concentrating on driving. The dirt had blocked her vision and by the time she slammed on the brakes, it was too late.

She found the phone on the passenger side floorboard. Three feet away but it might as well be a thousand. Her right arm was useless and her left couldn't reach it. She would perish only three feet from rescue like someone dying of thirst just short of an oasis.

The thing outside moved again, as if it were pacing. She couldn't make it out.

She looked again in the rearview mirror. Emily wasn't there.

She stared down at the wound, just visible in the radio light. Blood gushed down her leg. She counted the throbs. Eighty beats per minute. She'd have to slow her heart rate or she'd die soon. She had to be calm. No one would search for her for hours. Bill didn't care where she was and Jesse wouldn't worry until the afternoon. By that time she'd be dead.

She looked in the rearview mirror. Emily wasn't there.

The thing sat stationary on the bent hood. What was it? It moved closer to the windshield.

"Can you help me?"

No answer.

She found a pencil in the armrest cup holder. She stretched as far as she could toward the passenger seat floorboard. The pencil tapped against the cell phone. She sat back in the seat, exhausted from pain.

She thought she saw Jesse in the passenger side window. She had met him when she was a sophomore in high school. He was handsome, athletic, a football player, though extraordinarily shy for someone so popular. They would love each other until the end of time and would never leave each other's side. Never. After high school, he would play in college and she would go to nursing school. They'd marry. They'd have children. Jesse joined the Army. Without a scholarship, he had no other choice. He shipped out to Iraq three years ago. She'd wait.

Two years ago, he came back. He had only one arm and one and a half ears. He was hideous. She left him. She married Bill. They had Emily. Two months ago, she bumped into Jesse. She still loved him no matter how he looked. They met and made love. Then they met again. And again. Two hours ago, Bill slapped her and kicked her out of her own home.

She looked in the rearview mirror. Emily wasn't there.

The thing reared back on it hind legs and slammed into the shattered window with its front paws. The windshield bent in a few inches toward her. She screamed. A wolf. Gray and growling, poking its nose through a small hole in the windshield, its teeth clicking. A smell of wet fur and rotted meat. She drove the pencil into its snout and screamed as the beast yelped and backed away. It violently shook its head from side to side until the pencil flew from his soft wet nose. He pounced again. The windshield held, but just.

Jesse pounded on the passenger side window with his stump. He screamed her name. Bill smashed him with a rock, bloodying the half ear.

A rattlesnake slithered through the small hole in the windshield. Didn't snakes sleep at night? The wolf backed off, just visible now in the brown glow of the headlight. The snake slid down the cockeyed steering wheel and onto her lap. It twisted its head to look into her eyes. She held her breath as it opened its jaw wide to flash its fangs.

"They're lovely," she said.

It grinned and coiled around her leg. It stopped at the wound and flicked its tongue under the mini blood fountain. Satiated, it slid to the floor.

Jesse crashed hard into the window and beat viciously at it with his good arm. Bill grabbed him around the neck in a stranglehold.

She saw the "On Star" button above the mirror. She had let the free subscription run out a year ago. But still. When she pushed the button, the radio lights went out and the headlight went dark.

The wolf reared up and smashed through the windshield.

She looked in the rearview mirror. Emily wasn't there.

The Banshee of Strabane

"A banshee could be best described as a spirit or fairy in Gaelic folklore, whose appearance or wailing warns one that they will soon die. I have tolerated these specters in the past, for although their warnings are true harbingers of death, there is little the warned can do other than wait for my visit.

The most interesting thing about this story is not its inane and incredulous narrative or its shallow wordsmithing, but instead, the mystery of the Banshee's warning to the fair town of Strabane. Who is she warning? Why is she warning them? Are there to be more deaths? One can only hope, for there were far few in the tale.

Que sera. If nothing else, one can be reassured that a woman scorned must be taken seriously."

~ *G.R.*

Light wind bends the heather reverently toward the small group of construction workers who, with their foreman, stare curiously at the excavated patch of ground. The foreman speaks in a lovely, lucid baritone.

"Billy. Did you call the sheriff?"

129

"Aye. An hour away, Mike." Billy removes his hardhat and combs his greasy hair with splayed fingers. "So—what's the story of the banshee, Mike? Not much talk about it in Donegal, but I've heard the tune."

Mike nods and softly sings the first few lines of the ballad as if he were alone on the scarred berm.

Tell me the news of my sweet darlin' Mary.
The lass with the sweetest smile west of Derry.

He rubs his face to shed the fatigue of the day. "Most of the lads know the tale, but I can tell it again. I'd say it's appropriate considering the circumstances."

The setting sun flits off the small hill eerily lighting the seven men, their glow reflecting back to heaven, provisions for the stars later, as Mike's mother would tell him when she tucked him in as a boy.

"It was nearly a hundred years ago today, boys, 1853, or thereabouts. Our latest famine had nearly run its course and the good people of Eire waited patiently for the bloody Brits to proffer the next. Mary O'Dowd was sixteen that year and lived with her sickly ma, right here." Mike points to a small knoll now blocking the sun. "You boys razed the remains of the house this morning, as you know. Her dado had been dead four years that summer and so she and her mother leased their small acres for others to farm what they could of this rocky earth. What little rent they received barely sustained the girl and her ma, most of the coins passed on to Lord Compton for his due, may God roil his English soul in everlasting damnation."

"Amen," the boys say together.

"Her ma never quite recovered from the famine disease she contracted in '47 and so she would be with her daughter only a few short years more.

"At sixteen, Mary was a real beauty, yet seemed not to realize what she possessed, so shy she hung her head unattractively as she walked through town even when the lads paraded in front of her in hopes to catch her attention. The reticent child had soft, alabaster skin and gentle curves where God meant them. Her blue eyes burned through you though few had the pleasure, she always tracking her feet, like she was.

"It was said at the time that she was looking for a suitor to take her from her suffering, the mother then mad with disease of the brain and its malevolent imaginings. So it was no surprise the girl fell for a young peddler of potions and notions, his laudanum a favorite of the local constabulary and commissioners. Danny O'Brien was too handsome to be trusted, they said, but God help him, he possessed the gift of the talk, albeit mostly blarney and deception. But the young Mary's naiveté gave the girl no sense in the matter and she would have thrown herself in front of a dead-cart if the boy had desired such a thing.

"He came with his wares twice or thrice a year and each time he'd visit his Mary in the outskirts where the guardian angels set to catch their breath from helping the sinners of Strabane, two miles, there." Mike points toward the seashore.

"It wasn't a month later after his last courting, she announced they'd be wed a few weeks before the Lord Jesus's birthday. A happier girl you'd never seen, though I didn't know anyone personally who knew her then, me not born until the turn of the century, like I was.

"Well, Christmas came and went and the girl nearly died of the sorrow of the jilted bride. Mr. O'Brien was naught heard from after that, as if he never existed on the dear island. It was rumored he perished on a famine boat to America but there was no verifying that, you know, so many died, they did.

"There was no consoling the lass. She wandered into town a few times a year after that for supplies, but when her sainted mother succumbed to her retched malady, the young Miss O'Dowd never came back again. So distraught, she was over her wayward beau, she stayed out here in the gloom and mist until God in his mercy took her in his arms, thirty-six years ago, this month."

"And, so—was she the banshee?" Billy asks.

"Aye. She was that, and I swear on the very soul of the virgin mother to it, my boy. It was said when her mother died, the disease of the brain that affected the woman left her soul and leapt to Mary's. It was an awful thing, what the girl did to herself each night of her life until her ascension. A terrible thing, the orchestration of Beelzebub, it had to be, the suffering of that girl. Each night, a few hours past dusk, the wails and screams drifted on the north wind and worked toward the town like some fetid gas into the homes of the good folk. Many a summer, me blessed mother would close the shutters and suffer the heat rather than listen to the terrible keening. Sometimes if you concentrated doubly on the sound you could hear the accompanying cracks and pops that made me flinch and wince in me small bed, wondering when they'd stop. Dear Jesus I prayed for the west wind most nights, I tell you now.

"The town knew what the girl was up to, but like all good folk they minded their own business and let her be. They knew there was nary a soul on the emerald island that didn't have to fight their own demons just like the sorrowful lass fought hers. Yes, they did nothing and I believe it was for the best.

"For sixty-four years, Mary would come out at night on this very hill and scream to her God to explain to her why she was to suffer the torments and die a maiden when so many others had the joy of love. It was a terrible wail that filled the hollows and dales with its wolf-like mourning.

"Though sadly cruel, what made it worse, boys, were the lashes. Crack, crack, crack, you would hear in the space between wails. Crack, crack, crack. I wished to God I never heard the horrible sounds. The town knew it well; self-flagellation not uncommon to certain sects of the priesthood, but still it was a pox on the innocent town and on the innocent girl.

"Mary became subject of tales around the hearth and her suffering was put to song like the one I sang earlier. Children taunted her from outside her house though she never left her sanctuary save to keen at the night skies.

"In '08, Patrick Brennan and me risked the tormented woman's wrath and snuck up to the back of her house one evening. It was a bitch of a cold that night, and what do we see, but Mary O'Dowd, herself, then seventy years old, walking out to the hill in bare feet, wearing nothing but a white night dress. 'She must be daft,' Patrick says to me. I silently agreed as my own feet were numb. As soon as she crested the hill she flung her arms to God and screamed as if she were trying to burst the stars. A banshee wail that nearly split my eardrum.

"An hour, gentlemen. An hour, she screamed, stopping only to whip herself mercilessly with the cat-o'-nine tails, little fishhooks at the tips that tore into her flesh. At first, there were only thin, dark stains on her back, just visible in the waning moon, but then blood soaked the back of her nightdress in an obscene blotting that made me rightly sick to my stomach. Thank the Lord she finally stopped and worked her way back to the house. As she neared the door, Patrick coughed. She stopped to look at the thin grass where we lay, but we kept our mouths shut. She went inside and as we stood to leave she reappeared toting a shotgun. We ran down the hill like rabbits, but the boom hit us the same moment the rock salt did. Me arse and back was tender for a week later, by God.

"She died near the end of the war, finally free of her demons, but that wasn't the last we heard of her, if you believe the stories. Even now, it's said you can hear her screams, the banshee calls, riding the heavy mist, frightening the next generation and the next and the next, the children wondering of the loud cracks at night.

"By God, I have to make a worker's wages building the bosses' houses and developments, but I'd never tempt the phantoms and specters by living out here. Mind you lads, you follow my example. A woman so pained and tormented as she was would be of a mind to stay where she died.

"That's it boys. A woman scorned and a lifetime of unrequited love. That would be the all of it, what would make the girl go mad. That's what we all thought—until today."

Mike kneels on one knee and shoves aside some dirt from the patch of ground. One of the boys had turned on the headlights of the loader, the yellow light casting the men's shadows over the excavated patch. With his penknife, Mike pries a newborn's skull from the ground, shakes out the excess dirt and holds it up to the light.

Meth House

Published 2013, FWA, "It's A Crime" Anthology

"For your literary enjoyment we present Shirley, perhaps the most boring character ever conceived despite the millions of books and stories written over the ages. At seventy-seven years, I suspect I shall soon have her neck in my scythe dragging her down the fiery rabbit hole to her eventual maison permanente.

But in the meantime, our aged matron has somehow involved herself with a neighbor of suspect morals which could lead to the demise of someone.

Would that someone be collecting social security? I'll never tell."

~ G.R.

He had five pots cooking and three gassing on the makeshift tables that lined the walls of the garage. Usually, he kept lists and checked off each ingredient added so he didn't blow himself and the house to hell, but after two months in his meth lab he knew it all by heart. Like those guys that  spun plates on sticks, he was talented enough to multi-task eight pots at a time. She pushed him to produce more so they could move into a larger house with a bigger, better lab. It was hard to argue with her when you stepped back and counted the baggies full of crank.

He scraped off red phosphorus from the matchbox. He needed more of it and more lye and more acetone if he wanted to meet their quota. He walked over to the garage door and stood on his tip toes to stare out the little windows. She was still out on the sidewalk gabbing with the nosy neighbor. God, sometimes the bitch was useless as tits on a boar hog.

He hurried back to his work and began the gassing for another pot. The crystals formed delightfully at the bottom of the bottle. He crushed a few and snorted a small amount of the powder. The high was immediate and distracted him from pot number six where the lithium he had removed from several batteries earlier was reacting with the water violently and burning a small hole in the bottom of the plastic bottle.

* * *

Shirley's legs hurt from standing and from the arthritis, or Arthur-eye-tis, as her husband Arthur used to call it to be funny, you know, a play on words with his name, God rest his soul. But at seventy-seven she felt her age, especially when gossiping with her young neighbor from across the street, Brandy Hattaway.

Brandy's three year old, Nathan, wouldn't let go of his mother's leg and kept wiping the snot from his nose on his sleeve. Shirley opened her purse and handed him a tissue.

"Here you are, Nathan. Now blow your nose." He did so like a good boy.

"It's always running," Brandy said. She was thirty-two. She had never told Shirley her age but Shirley figured it out from the tattoo on the small of Brandy's back that read 1981. Shirley never liked the practice of tattooing your body. It was disgusting on men—let alone women. Only sailors wore them when she was young.

Cottony clouds blew by in the strong summer wind. She could smell the ocean on it even from ten miles away. She frowned at the two junk cars parked on the side of Brandy and Lucas's house. You'd think with all his free time he'd repair those eyesores.

"How's Lucas getting along, dear?" Shirley asked.

"Doesn't know what the hell to do with himself since he got out of prison. He's a mess, but they nearly killed him in there. Might look for something in sanitation, maybe, I don't know." Brandy slapped at Nathan who tugged at her shorts. "Stop that. Now go check on Hanna." The boy sniffled and walked toward the house.

"Well, a handsome man like him should be able to find something. My Arthur had a little trouble when we were first married in'54. All things will pass and all will be better. You'll see."

Talking about Arthur brought back the memory of their graduation and that dark, starry night outside Passaic. Oh, how she missed him. There was never another like him.

* * *

He mixed the ephedrine with the acetate, red phosphorous, ammonia nitrate, a little radiator coolant, and very little lithium. It already felt warm from the reaction. It was way too acidic so a little lye to change the pH and it was ready to cook. He thought about snorting a little more of the crystal when he noticed the small flame jutting out of the bottom of one of the plastic quart bottles. What the hell was that about?

* * *

Brandy lit a cigarette and offered one to Shirley knowing full well Shirley didn't smoke. Another disgusting habit the young seemed to embrace more and more lately.

"No thank you, dear." Shirley removed her car keys from her purse. "I have to be going. I think I'll do a little shopping, maybe go to the mall."

Brandy nodded and blew smoke from her nostrils. "Well you be good, Shirl. No stopping by bingo and checking out the geezers, girl. I'd better see what Nathan is—"

Both Shirley and Brandy screamed as the pressure wave from the explosion hit them. All of the windows and the front door blew out in an eruption of smoke and fire. The garage and the roof on the east side were in flames.

"Oh my goodness," Shirley said, adjusting her glasses.

Brandy stared at the conflagration for several seconds and then ran toward her house, yelling, "Oh, my babies!"

Shirley brushed off her skirt and then bent over to retrieve the car keys she had dropped during the explosion. She turned to stare at her ruined house. "The idiot," she said, shaking her head. It seemed like no matter who she hired for the lab they eventually screwed up with the usual disastrous results. Now she'd have to find another house and start all over again.

She carefully slid into the seat, started the car, and then adjusted the rearview mirror. It must have moved out of kilter from the explosion. She sighed, checked her hair in the mirror, and drove off.

The Execution of Claude Pictor

Second Place Fiction, 2009 Prescott Arizona Professional Writers Competition

"Claude Pictor is a student of executions, how they are delivered, the methods used, the morbid consequences of the blade, or rifle, or noose. He has plenty of time to research the subject, incarcerated as he has been for most of his life.

As you read along you may become confused and disoriented especially with dates and geographical settings. You are not alone. This tale reads like a Jackson Pollack canvas with little understood and nothing explained.

I would be brazen to say the author was under the influence when writing said piece and yet I believe his readers might be better off under the influence while reading said stories."

~ *G.R.*

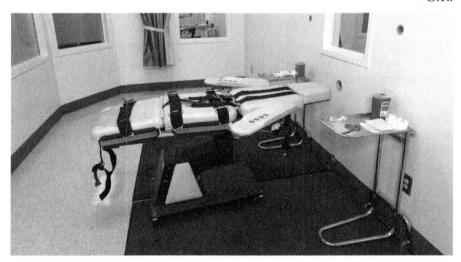

It didn't feel like an execution to Claude. The antiseptic smell of the small room, its walls painted a flat aquamarine hue, reminded Claude of the few times he had been in a hospital.

His executioners were as diligent, professional, and each as void of a pleasant disposition as any nurse who had ever administered their miracle concoction into his veins. These chemicals though, were hardly what anyone would describe as a miracle concoction, unless of course you were a relative of Claude's victim.

"This is to help with the IV insertion," the thinnest of his executioners said as he poked the hypodermic needle in Claude's arm.

"It won't leave a bruise will it, buddy?" Claude asked, trying to get a rise out of the resolute technician. Claude's sarcasm flew over the head of the man so he decided to omit any more attempts at levity.

It was a serious procedure after all, and the man was just trying to relieve Claude of a little pain by educating him on the process. It wasn't necessary. Claude had always been somewhat obsessed with executions over time and knew a great deal about them. All three of his executioners and the ten or twelve witnesses outside the small death room would be surprised to know just how much knowledge he had of the process.

After all, he'd been in prison fourteen years on a first-degree murder conviction for a crime he didn't commit and ten more for one he did, which gave plenty of idle time to read about nearly everything, including the marvelous art of killing criminals for the state. And then of course, there was his past.

Claude had burned the entire procedure into his brain long ago, ten years ago to be exact, right after he killed the prison guard, because he knew the good State of Florida would eventually have to discontinue the barbaric ritual of boiling the brains and innards of their most debauched criminals and progress to lethal injection.

Claude's thoughts were distracted momentarily as the cute one of the three executioners strapped Claude's arms to boards that jutted obliquely out of the top of the gurney. It gave the impression of a crucifixion with Claude's arms outstretched above his head. The young man seemed a little too fastidious with the plastic tie wraps.

"C'mon son," Claude said. "Ease up a little, huh? Can't feel my damn fingers. Afraid I might get loose and toothbrush you or something?"

Claude was referring to the creative way he had stabbed a prison guard with a sharpened toothbrush in the hapless guard's eye. The squishy noise the homemade shiv made as it passed through the eyeball and penetrated the brain still made Claude go all goose bumpy.

The cute technician's eyes widened with fear and he loosened the straps slightly, prompting a huge sigh of relief from Claude.

Claude could read eyes. He'd had that ability for what seemed like forever. The fear in the cute executioner's eyes was the easiest of the three to read. The others, a little more difficult, but the thin one's eyes expressed a good amount of empathy, while the third man, 'Mr. overweight for his height,' showed what Claude assumed was derisiveness. Yes, the fat one would look forward to Claude's eventual demise, but would wax melancholy without the suffering.

Claude sure knew how to read them. Just like the guard with the toothbrush adornment, he read all their eyes. Maybe that's why he stabbed Billy Lang in the eye, because Claude saw in Billy that look of condescending superiority. How could he let someone get away with that? He couldn't, and he didn't.

* * *

"Your honor," the elegant defense lawyer emoted. "I am not asking the court to believe my client innocent of the charges brought against him. He freely admits that he killed the guard without conscience, without remorse, without regard to the feelings of the victim's relatives left behind to mourn. What I am saying is that he is not alone to blame for the murder. Some responsibility must be leveled on the state for what they imposed on my client with fourteen years of injustice!"

The defense attorney flailed his arms to dramatize his eloquent rhetoric. Claude just smiled ever so slightly and folded his arms across his chest as in an act of defiance more so than to keep warm in the cold musty court.

"Yes—yes, we've gone over that numerous times, counselor," the judge said. "We don't disagree with you that your client was unjustly convicted of a murder he didn't commit. That is not what this trial is about. This trial, counselor, as you know, is primarily about the murder of a prison guard. A murder your client admits to. Is it not?"

"It is your honor. What I am asking is for the court to agree that my client was not a murderer until fourteen years of incarceration shaped him from a good honest citizen into a monstrous animal. He did not commit the deed. You—the state—the citizens of this city—the government—they killed that guard just as surely as my client. Their forced imprisonment of the defendant created that monster, and they, not my client should be found guilty!"

The judge applauded.

"Bravo—bravo, counselor, a marvelous performance, but the facts are the facts and all your rhetoric and flowery prose cannot change facts. Give us facts. Give us something that will prove your client innocent of killing his guard. Give us facts that will prove the state, and not his malevolence, employed him to remove a human being from this world and leave a grieving widow and four young, impressionable children to mourn their irreplaceable loss. Show us that, counselor."

The lawyer shook his head. "I cannot. I ask you only to judge my client objectively. Had it been your son imprisoned for a crime he did not commit, would you not decide differently?"

The trial was a farce in Claude's opinion. He knew the outcome just as sure as everyone in the enormous courtroom knew. No judge would allow a person of his perversions, his evil mind, loose on a god-fearing respectable society. A good thing too, for if they ever did make the mistake of releasing him into the community he would wreak a plethora of crime the city had never seen.

Good for them. They reaped what they had sewn. Fourteen years earlier, he walked down a singularly desolate street after having a quite physical and noisy session of lovemaking with a particularly attractive young maiden in the tall grass of a meadow. At least he thought she was a maiden. Perhaps not, but regardless, they parted amiably.

So, it was a surprise to him when he was arrested for the murder of the deflowered maiden. Very surprising. It was difficult for Claude to defend his innocence as well as explain his whereabouts at the time of the homicide.

The trumped up charges held spectacularly in court. The best defense lawyer in the country, who coincidentally now defended Claude in the murder of the guard, could not be expected to save his worthless hide from prison.

Claude was sentenced to life imprisonment for the murder of his young lover. Only the memory of her enthusiastic lovemaking kept his sanity for those fourteen years.

He learned much while in prison; arts, skills and most importantly, how to defend himself from others intent on his submission. He learned fast. He learned well. He learned the numerous ways to kill a human being and after years of animalistic survival, he used his skill to remove from earth, a particularly annoying and condescending guard.

* * *

The thin executioner, Claude reckoned, was in charge of the procedure. The two others acted only on orders from him. The man slipped one of the two IVs into the ports the fat technician had installed in Claude's veins earlier. What a sight Claude must seem to the witnesses watching from the adjacent viewing area. How disappointing it will be for them to watch him fall asleep. For after all, that is what it will seem, a sweet, comfortable drift into sleep.

Out of the corner of his eye, Claude saw the widow of the eye impaled guard, sitting quietly, unemotionally, in her seat. He half expected her to mouth the word thank you to him, for he had made her a millionaire when he snuffed out that ridiculously stupid guard. The ungrateful bitch.

After the state decided, yes indeed, they had imprisoned Claude unfairly for the murder of his lover, they graciously awarded 2.3 million dollars to him as retribution for the fourteen years of hell they put him through.

After paying his lawyer, Claude graciously turned the rest, over a million, to the widow of Billy Lang. It's true Claude's real intention was to have the court see this gesture as proof of his rehabilitation, but in the end, it did nothing for his cause, and they sentenced him to death, regardless.

The stupid bitch. The least she could have done ten years ago was ask the court to spare his life.

Thin guy leaned over the gurney to talk to Claude. "I want you to know that you will feel no pain. The solution we're running now is just saline. When the warden gives me the signal, I will inject five grams of sodium pentothal. This is a barbiturate that will render you unconscious. Once you are out, the other two chemicals, pancuronium bromide and potassium chloride will complete the procedure to expiration. It's a simple procedure and you'll feel no pain."

Claude jerked his arms and legs up against the gurney restraints frightening the technician, who backed away.

"Restraints are good," Claude said loudly. "Otherwise you'd be pulling those scissors out of your head, junior." Claude smiled. He still had his menacing touch. "Turn around, junior. I bet you shit your pants." Claude smiled again until he saw the doctor enter the room. He was there to pronounce him dead, later. It was the same as it always was. Each time identical, only the method changed.

Claude was indeed an expert in executions. He knew them all. The messiest was beheading, a favorite of both the East and the West until the seventeenth century. The axe, no matter its size and weight, was a miserable and inefficient method at best to execute a man. So many times, it took several blows to decapitate the poor soul.

The guillotine was a much-improved method of beheading, and in Claude's opinion, still the most humane administration of state vengeance.

Hanging still surfaced in some countries, including the United States, but there was always the risk of the condemned suffering a slow, painful death. Cruel and unusual for sure, Claude thought.

However, in Claude's opinion, electrocution was the cruelest way to kill. No one knew just how painful it was. Well—no one other than himself.

* * *

There would be no surprise outcome in the trial. Claude had resigned himself for the guilty verdict issued by the sagacious judge and jury. No matter. He had no regrets of his past, just an overwhelming fear of the future.

"Will the defendant please rise," the judge ordered. Claude and his lawyer stood. The judge continued. "I must first commend your counselor, Marcus Tullius Cicero, on the exemplary defense he presented in your case. He put forth a good argument that the state was somewhat responsible for creating the malevolence that controls your very being. However, as I stated previously, the facts show two things: One, that you are innocent of the murder of the vestal virgin, Tiberia Aemilianus, and two, that you are guilty of murdering the centurion Lucius Capito. With those facts in mind, the jurors have awarded you, Claudius Pictorus, the sum of 100 sesterius for your wrongful arrest in the first case.

"In the second case the jurors sentence you to death for the murder of Lucius Capito. With the power bestowed on me by the emperor Caesar, I sentence you to be executed by beheading, one hour before dusk, tomorrow. So it is said, so it will be done."

Claude spoke up. "Senator, may I be allowed to speak?"

The judge nodded. "Yes—briefly."

Claude smiled and continued.

"Senator, I wish to bequeath 50 sesterius of my award to the widow of the guard I am accused of murdering and the other 50 to Masavo.

Masavo was the executioner known to use a very dull sword for beheadings unless bribed ahead of time, in which case he would lop the head off in one tremendous blow, alleviating any unnecessary pain for the condemned.

The senator nodded approvingly. "A wise choice, young Claudius."

* * *

The time of repentance had arrived for Claude, but he felt no atonement. He had been through this so many times in the past that the whole ritual of execution bored him.

First in Denmark, where the brute sliced through his neck with a double-sided broad axe. Then the beheading in Rome, where the sword was thankfully razor sharp. The rest of his executions, faint memories. The French guillotine, the hanging in England, the firing squad in Spain, the electric chair in New York and now, lethal injection in sunny Florida, and each for murdering a guard.

Perhaps in the future no guard would be posted and Claude might live into his senior years, but he doubted it. More likely, there would be a new and even more humane method of disposing of society's dregs. Perhaps vaporization? Perhaps. Then only a janitor would be needed to sweep away the remains.

The thin technician hung up the phone. Obviously, the warden had not granted a stay. The fat technician grinned as the thin one pressed the button to start the procedure.

Claude stared spellbound at his lower body as skin melted off his bones, leaving only a chalky white skeleton on the gurney. It was just his imagination of course. The same vision he had each time before the executioner delivered the fatal blow. It was a vision he'd endure through eternity, as he continued to live his virtual hell.

J.J. WHITE

Beneath the Wintry Sky

First Place winner Missouri Writers Guild 2011
Short Story Competition
First Place winner 2012 Oregon Writers Colony Contest
Second Place winner Writers/Editors 2012
Short Story Competition

"This twisted tale has many deaths, though the corpses are anonymous and generally just used as a writing trick to set tone and setting. Not beneath the dignity of our author as he often uses tricks to hide his lack of writing skills and intolerable prose.

For the millionth time, it seems, the author uses the moniker, Joe, for his main character's name, as if there are no other men's names he could use despite owning a computer with access to the internet.

I digress. Joe is an American soldier in Belgium and the war is nearly over. Despite his instinct to keep himself out of battle and safe he throws caution to the wind to procure a small Christmas tree for his foxhole. While procuring said tree he comes across a young German soldier also searching for a tiny tannenbaum. If I were the author, there would be two dead soldiers and two uncut Christmas trees, but I am not the author and he has other ideas. I hate sad endings. Sad for me, anyway."

~ *G.R.*

Snow fell from an ash gray sky, nearly invisible until a few feet from the ground, the flakes dusting odd-shaped drifts dyed brown from the piss, shit and blood of the 292nd infantry regiment.

He had slept only four hours in five days of constant battles, his side surrendering St. Vith back to the Panzer divisions. Window dressing for the Reich, one success in a lost war, with only one conclusion, the end of their noble quest. The Nazis were delaying the inevitable and taking as many of the enemy with them as they could.

A shell from a Kraut eighty-eight exploded about fifty feet from Joe's foxhole, an eruption of dirt covering the fresh snow. There was plenty of snow, and sleet, and ice, all penetrating their sleeping bags, coats, and boots, while preserving the mangled bodies of their comrades, blessedly saving the living from the smell of the dead. He'd had enough of death, and enough of war. Why did civilized men capable of understanding mathematics, building cathedrals, and conquering disease, think they needed to club each other to death for a little land?

Joe had shot his first enemy soldier over a year ago. He had squeezed the trigger as if he were holding a baby bird, the rifle nearly jumping out of his hands as the distant silhouette collapsed to the earth. He thought of the dead soldier as an infant held by his parents over the crib, a toddler chasing playmates through high grass, a young man kissing his sweetheart as he boarded his train to eternity.

Those thoughts stopped after a few months of war. Joe felt none of them now. The enemy was faceless and nameless. He was eliminating someone intent on eliminating him. That's all it was. Anything else and you'd blow your brains out.

Kowalski threw the bottle across the foxhole to Joe. He wasn't expecting the toss and spilled some on his uniform.

"Dumb Polack," Joe said. "Don't they play any baseball in Jersey? You throw like a little girl."

It was Christmas brandy from Camden's girlfriend or lover or mother, who the hell knew. Camden wouldn't need it anyway, buried in a shallow grave two miles north of their entrenchment. Joe passed the bottle to Corporal Johansson who took a quick swig and handed it to Paul Santini. A goddamn League of Nations foxhole. Kowalski got the bottle back from Santini and held it out in salute. "To Jake Camden, God rest his soul." Santini made the sign of the cross. "And," Kowalski continued, "to a Merry Christmas and a Happy New Year."

"Yeah," Santini said. "Just like home, except there ain't no food, no family, no presents and no tree. Other than that, it's the same."

Santini pulled broken Christmas tree cookies from a sack and passed them around. "A little stale and broke to hell, but better than nothing, right Sarge?"

Joe nodded and nearly broke a tooth on a cookie trunk. It was a six-hour time difference between Belgium and Vermont. Kathy would be helping her parents start the Christmas dinner. Afterwards, they would stand by the tree and toast Joe and pray for his safety. He wondered where they got their tree from this year. Kathy's letters took months to get to him. She probably thought he was dead unless the Army was keeping the mess in Belgium secret.

The snow stopped as suddenly as it had started. Small black bugs crawled out from Santini's cookie sack. Welcome to our world, Joe thought and threw the rest of his cookie away.

Three years ago, he drove twenty miles to Shrewsbury to find the perfect Christmas tree. The Frasier Firs were at just the right height. The perfect tree for the in-laws. He and Kathy had made love quietly in her old bedroom, each wondering if it would be their last Christmas together. That gave him an idea. He stood, put on his helmet and strapped his carbine over his back.

"You know what we need?" he said.

"Betty Grable," Kowalski said.

"Besides that. We need a Christmas tree." He pointed to the woods. "There's a whole forest of 'em out there. Keep my seat warm." He pulled a small hatchet from his pack.

"You're gonna get yourself shot for a tree?" Santini asked.

"Yeah. I mean no. One of those eighty-eights hits in here it's goodbye Charlie, anyway. What's the difference?" And with that, he climbed out of the foxhole and ran bent over, holding his helmet on his head as he made a beeline to the forest, about a hundred yards away. The constant artillery barrage of the last two days had left few trees near the edge to choose from so Joe pushed further in until the woods were so thick they blotted out what was left of the setting sun through the heavy fog.

There it was, a four-foot spruce near the bottom of a small gully, the branches heavy with snow. He took the hatchet from his coat and after shaking the snow off the tree, began hacking at the trunk.

A few ration cans and some of Santini's stale cookies hanging from the thin branches and they'd have their own Christmas tree for their hole. Maybe *Stars and Stripes* would send a reporter. He could imagine the headline: "Four unlucky bastards blown up with their Christmas tree."

He stopped to light a cigarette. About thirty feet away, a German soldier sawed on a similar tree with a large knife. Their eyes met as Joe flicked his Zippo. He missed the tip of the cigarette with the flame by two inches.

Joe swung his rifle around and aimed first at the soldier's head, then the chest. Light pressure on the trigger, ready to squeeze, but he didn't. It surprised Joe as much as it did the Kraut. The German fumbled with his rifle but somehow managed to get it into firing position. He was just a kid.

Hell of a thing to die for, Joe thought, but there were worse ways to go and his intentions had been good. He hoped someone would tell Kathy the truth.

A gray squirrel jumped from one tree to the next behind the nervous German. It startled him enough that his Mauser shook. Then the man took a breath and yelled something at Joe that could have been anything. Joe understood a little German but Johansson was the only one fluent and he was a million miles away and drunk on stolen brandy.

Joe lowered his gaze to the soldier's tree. The boy hadn't made much progress with the knife. Maybe the Krauts didn't supply hatchets to their men when they fought in dense forests. It sounded like something Hitler would do.

Joe gently placed his rifle against a charred stump and then pointed to his hatchet. The soldier seemed to understand and nodded, so Joe picked it up and cleaved what was left of the trunk of his little tree with two mighty hacks. He held the tool out to the soldier. "Looks like you're having a tough time with that knife." He threw the hatchet to the boy's feet, where it sunk in the snow.

The soldier fished it out and began chopping at the base of his own small Tannenbaum, never taking his eyes off Joe. A couple of times Joe thought the guy might hack his foot off but the tree finally came loose of the trunk.

Joe walked over to him and the soldier immediately had his rifle up and aimed. The snow began to fall again, small flakes resting on the boy's long lashes. How old was he? Fifteen? Sixteen? Old enough and nervous enough to kill, he guessed.

The boy tried to hand the hatchet back to Joe, but Joe shook his head.

"You keep it, Hans. You need it more than I do."

Joe went back to the stump and picked up his rifle and the Christmas tree. He had walked away a few steps when the boy soldier said, *"Frohliche Weihnachten."*

Joe smiled, turned, then saluted lazily to him. "Merry Christmas to you too, buddy."

The Zodiac Killer Pizza Club

Published 2010 Helium.com

"What is it about serial killers that pique my fancy as well as my curiosity? Is it the anonymity of the culprits, the blatant arrogance, the cold steel delivery of the death blow, the sheer number of victims?

Yes.

There has been two infamous examples of serial killers who have never been caught, one being Jack the Ripper, a coward who preyed upon helpless women and, of course, the Zodiac, The genius of Northern California who sent cryptic clues to the police after supplying innocent fodder for my quiver.

Our author has woven fiction into fact as only he could, tarnishing the stellar reputation of my heartless protégé.

Oh well, read at your discretion, though I suspect a perusal of Wikipedia *would suffice."*

~ G.R.

It's unusually dark on the campus grounds as I work my way across damp grassy medians to my car through the faculty parking lot. Ten minutes earlier, the police called, insisting I stay outside the lecture hall until they, or the campus police, arrived to secure my safety. I didn't listen. Instead, I decided to walk to the parking lot. I was exposed either way, standing alone outside a locked hall or walking in the dark to my car.

My lecture, ironically, was on serial killers and how CAT scans prove they all have some type of physical abnormality of the brain. I'm not a medical doctor, but I have years of experience trying to catch one particularly clever killer that some say must also have this malady. After the three murders earlier today, the police are convinced I will be next.

I see the Mercedes ahead, parked alone under a lamppost. The lamp is burned out. The reason I parked under it is because the light makes it easier to find, and it deters young thieves. Better safe than sorry.

I press the button on the key, but I must still be too far away since I don't hear the familiar beep-beep reassuring me the doors are unlocked and waiting for their distinguished owner.

It's only fifty paces farther when I hear the unmistakable clomp of heavy footsteps behind. I stare straight ahead as the headlights finally flash when I thumb the electronic key.

The footsteps grow louder and increase in pace. Someone is trotting now, seemingly not sure whether to walk or run. I reach for the door handle just as I feel a hand on my shoulder. "Professor Larkin."

* * *

Between December 1968 and October 1969, a man who called himself the Zodiac Killer murdered two men and three women in and around Northern California for no apparent reason. He has never been caught but as it turned out, the man's horrific killing spree dramatically improved my academic and professional career.

Like most serial killers, Zodiac liked to leave little clues for the police to help them in their feeble attempts to capture him. Since he wasn't caught, one can assume the attempts were indeed feeble or Zodiac would still be serving out a life sentence, wouldn't he?

It wasn't like he didn't try to get captured. He published letters confessing those five murders as well as twenty-six more and he even wrote his real name down. The catch being the letters were cryptograms that the best cryptologists in the country were unable to decipher. I know. I'm one of them.

The Zodiac's first cryptogram, a 408 symbol puzzle, was cracked by amateur ciphers Donald and Betty Harden of Salinas. However, Zodiac lied when he promised the puzzle revealed his identity. The deciphered letter revealed nothing, other than showing the Zodiac was a genius who couldn't spell.

Two cryptograms he sent later were the ones I was interested in. One, a 340 character cipher supposedly revealed details of who he murdered and when he murdered them, while the other, a note received April 20, 1970 read, "My name is . . .," followed by a thirteen character cipher. They both remain unsolved.

Hence, the formation of the Zodiac Killer Pizza Club three years ago, created to have another go at the maniacal genius' ciphers and finally reveal his name.

A little about me, first. In 1969 I was 29 years old and an assistant professor of mathematics at Stanford University. My specialty was cryptology, the study of ciphers, including the encryption and decryption of algorithms. In layman terms, I convert gibberish into ordinary information or plain text. Since the Zodiac murders, it has been my job to teach others how to break codes.

When the San Francisco police department realized they lacked the expertise needed to crack the Zodiac's ciphers, they hired me. Although I was unable to accomplish my deciphering tasks for the authorities, I received national recognition for my attempts and went on to a successful career as a consultant for the NSA, CIA, and the FBI. Now in the autumn of my career, I am back at Stanford as a professor emeritus in the mathematics department.

Too much about me, I know. Back to the Pizza Club. It consists of four senior citizens, me being the oldest at 70. Two women, Greta Johansson and Maggie Washburn, were also cryptologists and like me worked for the government during and even after the cold war, deciphering the codes and secrets of the United States' many enemies. They have both since retired.

The fourth member, Max Stadler, was a detective with the San Francisco Police Department at the time of the Zodiac murders. Max is obsessed with solving the cold case and that was the reason he joined our group. He's not a qualified cryptologist but he has kept up our enthusiasm in our quest and besides, he usually pays for the pizza.

We meet twice a month at O'Malley's, a local bar that doesn't mind if we order pizza to complement the pitchers of beer we polish off in our pursuit of the infamous Zodiac Killer's identity.

We met recently. Greta arrived on time, punctual as ever, looking nothing like her sixty-two years. The attractive Swede, her back straight as a board against her chair, always proper, always meticulously dressed, her black hair glistening in the candlelight. Always so—European.

Each time I saw her, my reverie took me back to Washington and our clandestine rendezvous' at the Omni, her 33-year-old body pulsing rhythmically under me.

Ah—Greta. I sometimes wondered if she told her husband Oskar of our affair. I can imagine the scene. "Herbert and I have made love, Oskar. I am sorry to tell you this and I will not blame you if you are angry." And then the emotionless Oskar would reply. "I am not upset. If this is your pursuit then I will not interfere. I understood when we married that all could not be perfect. I expect you will be discreet, Greta."

And we were, as were Maggie and me. She, another workplace romance of about the same length of time between 1980 and 1985. Maggie, the complete opposite of the prim and proper Greta.

Their reactions so different, Greta with her pained face and quiet squeaks, while Maggie screamed first my name, then God's, sounding more like she was giving birth than exhibiting the throes of ecstasy.

Both were wonderful and exciting for a forty something cryptologist like myself, but the initial thrill wore off quickly, and now it's been almost twenty-five years since we were lovers. Still, we remain friends.

Then there is Max Stadler, short and stocky like Maggie, his spiked hair adorning a large head supported by an invisible neck. The career cop, determined to bring his man to justice even forty years after the crime, extemporizing for the Pizza Club the only way he can, as a cheerleader.

How many times have we met where the girls and I suffered over the meaning of a symbol while Max nodded in agreement as if he had a clue of what an algorithm was. But like I said, Max bought the pizzas. An investment he hoped paid off with the identity of the killer.

Although in three years of meetings we had not broken the entire code, we were still rewarded with bits and pieces by our steady, intricate pursuit, leaving us tantalizingly close to a key that solved the mystery.

Our club drew quite a bit of media attention recently when Max announced that we identified one name in the 340 symbol cipher, Michael Mageau, a July 4, 1969 victim. The two m's in his name were the key. Once we had the m's, we guessed the rest of the name. So apparently, Zodiac had listed his victims' names, but unfortunately, we couldn't decipher any of the others.

Up until our last meeting.

* * *

Midnight, July 5, 1969, Darlene Ferrin drove Michael Mageau to the Blue Rock Springs Golf Course in Vallejo, California to—well, to make out, obviously, as any healthy young man and woman would do on a lovely dark night.

A car pulled up behind them, its lights illuminating the inside of Darlene's car. Then it left as suddenly as it had arrived and the lovers went back to doing what lovers do, until minutes later when the car returned.

The Zodiac stepped out of his car, shone a flashlight in their faces, then shot them both three times. Mageau survived the attack despite being shot in the face, neck and chest. Ferrin died.

*   *   *

Maggie arrived at O'Malley's a half-hour late for our meeting. The pizza had arrived just a few minutes earlier, which helped temper our frustration at her tardiness.

As usual, the pizza was topped differently on each quarter. From our initial meeting three years ago, it was obvious the four of us could not agree on the same pizza so we compromised by having each quarter topped with our own choice.

My section had mushrooms, Max ordered beef, Maggie, pepperoni, and the lovely Swede always asked for anchovies. The pizza looked like one of those game pieces in Trivial Pursuit, each section a different color.

While Maggie sat, I poured the beer. The lager felt wonderful going down my parched throat. Greta pointed her pizza slice at Maggie. "In 73 meetings, Maggie, this is the first time you have been late. Shall we assume you have a reason?"

"You may, dear Greta, for I have a reason. When one has solved the key to our friend Zodiac's cipher, one may be as goddamn late as one wants."

Max's eyes lit up as if he were hit with a cattle prod. "What did you say, Maggie?"

I stopped mid-bite. "You're joking."

"I am not joking. It's binary. The key is binary. Each letter, each symbol, each nonsensical mark our sick friend scratched on his enigmatic nonsense can be deciphered with a simple binary number."

"Let's hold up, Maggie," Max said, a piece of beef lodged between his two front teeth. "You guys have gone that route before. Last year, I think. Each letter was assigned numbers and it didn't help at all, right?"

Maggie nodded. "Yes. Ones and zeros and yes the cipher still made no sense until ..." Maggie chomped on her pizza slice to let us suffer a bit.

"Yes—until?" Greta asked.

Maggie swallowed and drank from her pilsner glass before answering.

"Until I used Boolean Algebra."

"Boolean Algebra," Greta said, looking as if she understood completely. "Yes."

Maggie pulled one of the copies of the 340-letter cipher from a pile we always kept on the table and pointed at some letters with her pen.

"Here. Let's take Mr. Mageau's name. M first. All right, start with the letter A."

Greta spoke, "Zero, zero, zero, one."

"Yes," Maggie said. "Now we know the symbol he uses, the triangle, is an A or the second letter in the name but ignore that for now. Like I said, start with M or the first letter of Mageau. Assume each word as an entity in itself so the M is . . ."

"Twelve letters ahead," I said.

"Yes, twelve. But to find the M you must add the Boolean equivalent for the number twelve and then . . ."

Maggie spent the next hour showing us how she turned the name Mageau and its Zodiac symbols into binary algorithms.

The excitement at the table was palpable, with hardly anyone touching their pizza or beer. After Maggie finished, I stood, walked around the table and kissed the moist lips that used to excite me in the secret hotel room so many years ago. "Maggie," I said. "You are a remarkable woman. A genius."

"Yes, yes," Max said. "And if Professor Larkin is finished romancing the genius then can we keep going with the code? Let's figure the whole thing out tonight. What are we waiting for? If this bastard is still alive, I want to see him hang."

I looked over to Maggie. "You tell him, dear."

Maggie rubbed Max's buzz-cut hair. "Max—it will take weeks. A little at a time but we'll get 'er done big fella. Patience."

"Well how about the thirteen symbol name cipher," Max said. "Let's do that first."

I raised my hands. "It's late, Max. We don't have any letters in the name cipher. It would take until morning. Let's do a few words near the Mageau name, where we do have letters, and save the rest. I'll work on some symbols on the name cipher in the morning and when we meet tomorrow night, we'll complete the rest."

"Okay, Herb—sounds good. But how about if I go to the television station and have them film us while we solve his name."

I looked questioningly at the girls, who both shrugged and I said. "Why not? We deserve a little publicity after all our hard work. All right, tomorrow night—early. Let's see if we can make the six o-clock news. But before we go, let's tackle a few words."

The words we tackled turned out to be another name, Betty Lou Jensen.

* * *

December 20, 1968, Betty Lou Jensen and David Farady went on a first date just inside the Benicia City limits. After visiting a friend and eating at a local restaurant, the teenagers turned down Lake Herman Road and parked David's Rambler in a small gravel turnaround the locals knew as a well-known lover's lane.

Around 11 p.m., a car pulled beside them. Zodiac got out with a pistol and ordered David and Betty Lou out of the car. While he shot David in the head, Betty Lou ran away. From thirty feet, Zodiac shot her five times in the back. Stella Borges, who lived nearby, found the bodies minutes later.

* * *

Max didn't wait for the next afternoon to contact the media. I watched him on the noon news explain how the four of us had broken Zodiac's code and later that evening would solve the name of the infamous Zodiac Killer.

I called Max immediately and chastised him for jumping the gun but fortunately it worked out since I was informed a few hours later that I would be giving an impromptu lecture that night at the university.

Max, Greta, Maggie and I agreed to meet at 8 p.m. and solve the name cipher in time for the eleven o'clock news. After forty agonizing years, Max could finally close the case that had haunted him since October 11, 1969, when Paul Lee Stine was shot and killed by the Zodiac in the Presidio Heights' neighborhood. It would all be over soon.

* * *

Maggie Washburn unlocked the front door of her townhouse and juggled two bags of groceries as she walked over the threshold. She had lived there since retiring from the NSA, enjoying its proximity to downtown.

She placed the groceries on the kitchen table and quickly lit a Marlboro Light. She knew the habit might be the reason the attractive Professor Larkin no longer took a sexual interest in her. The memory made her sigh as she blew out a long puff of smoke.

Zodiac walked out of the dining room, lifted his pistol and shot Maggie three times in the head.

* * *

Greta shut off the six o'clock news and shuddered, thinking of the pressure the media would place on the Pizza Club later that night when they presented the solved serial killer's puzzle. It would be a relief to have the solution after three long years, but she would dearly miss the meetings and her wonderful companions.

She sat up in the bed and bumped her head on the muzzle of a gun. Zodiac only used the one bullet, as there was little doubt the attractive Swede was dead.

* * *

Max drove quickly up his driveway to his 2400 square foot ranch style house. He and Millie had only paid ninety thousand for it in 1982. It would sell easily for half a million.

As he shut off the car, he couldn't stop himself from smiling. Tomorrow it would be over and if the goddamn punk was still alive, Max would track him down.

A sharp crack startled Max. It came from the back seat. Max peered into the rearview mirror and reached for his Glock .40 on the seat next to him. He saw two eyes stare back at him as Zodiac put two rounds in the back of the retired detective's square head.

* * *

"Professor Larkin."

The voice startles me as I open the door to the Mercedes. I turn quickly and see a campus police officer illuminated from the dome light in my car.

"Yes. What is it—Officer—Mendes." I said after reading his nametag.

"Sir. The police have asked me to escort you to the campus police office immediately. They're worried, you know, about the Zodiac guy, after what happened earlier with your friends."

I nod. Yes, I knew. Max's enthusiasm to announce to the world the solution of the Zodiac cipher had brought the killer out of hiding. Now the monster was eliminating the Zodiac Killer Pizza Club before they could reveal his name. Poor Max. Poor Maggie. Poor beautiful, sensitive Greta.

"Yes of course, officer. I'll follow you in my car."

"Thank you sir," Mendes said, looking relieved. "My cruiser is right over there." He points to a campus police car across the parking lot.

I throw a stack of papers on the passenger seat and start the car. Before I place the gear in drive, I notice the Zodiac's thirteen-letter name cipher on top of the stack. I look at it carefully and smile. The thirteen blanks for the Zodiac's name are filled in. I failed to mention to the Pizza Club that I had solved the Zodiac's identity.

Oh well, I'll never be able to reveal the name to the public.

I can't—since it's my name.

CPSIA information
Printed in the USA
LVOW04s1612261

415836LV0

0615 861616